PAWZ for THOUGHT

Animal Tails

Janet Patterson

Grosvenor House
Publishing Limited

This book is published by
Grosvenor House Publishing Ltd
Link House
140 The Broadway, Tolworth, Surrey, KT6 7HT.
www.grosvenorhousepublishing.co.uk

A CIP record for this book
is available from the British Library

Paperback ISBN 978-1-83615-505-8

LIST OF CONTENTS

PART ONE: Animal Tails   **1**

The Wild One   3

The Pigeon and the Nightingale   15

Love on a Bus   25

The Great Escape   29

Bruno's Lament   57

The Buffaloes are Gone   85

Spanish Fly   87

The Matador   95

PART TWO: The Collection   **105**

Old Tom and the Half-Dead   107

Bobby   119

The Gold Coach   123

Meeting with a Stranger   127

The Torture Chamber   131

The House by the River   133

The Four Seasons   139

The Watchmaker   141

Casablanca   147

The Mystery Woman   161

Queenager   193

PART THREE: Living History   195

Life in La Herradura   199

Joaquim's Story   205

Maria   209

Paco and the Gypsies   213

Shipwreck in La Herradura Bay   215

Miguel Hernández – A Poet of the People   221

The Sixties   227

Preface

I always used to wonder why people published collections. Why didn't they just write a book? Now I know.

Having written several articles and short stories that had been published in local magazines over the past few years, I realized that, if I were to be beamed up, my stories would be lost to posterity. So I gathered up my scattered works as a mother hen gathers her chicks under her wings, and here they are for your delectation.

Part One is comprised of animal stories, featuring cats and dogs, a bull and a polar bear who raps, Percy the pigeon and a fly who disobeys his mother. They fall under a new category that I have just invented, 'the Adult Child.'

The middle section, 'The Collection,' is just that, a mishmash of short stories with a variety of themes. 'Old Tom' is about a tramp who goes to the church graveyard in order to enjoy his supper in peace. To his surprise, he meets the Half Dead, who entertain him throughout the night. Until the cock crows.

'Living History,' (Part Three) is a series of articles I wrote for a magazine about the Spanish Civil War and life during Franco's dictatorship. They are based on interviews with Spanish people who had been persuaded to talk about their personal experiences. Because there were atrocities committed on both sides during and after the war, those involved have agreed to a Pact of Silence. People were at first reluctant to talk to us, until they realized that we were not going to argue with them or judge them.

I hope you enjoy reading these stories as much as I have enjoyed writing them.

PART ONE

Animal Tails

The Wild One   3

The Pigeon and the Nightingale   15

Love on a Bus   25

The Great Escape   29

Bruno's Lament   57

The Buffalo are gone   85

Spanish Fly   87

The Matador   95

The Wild One

The zoo was abuzz with excitement. A wild lion was being shipped from Africa to stay at the lion house for a couple of months. It was part of an experiment to see how a wild animal would adapt to life in captivity. At the end of his stay, he would be returned to his native country, along with a domesticated lion from the zoo on a sort of exchange programme. The whole event would be filmed by David Attenborough and shown on the BBC.

The females were all aflutter:

'Have you heard the news?' asked Zelda. 'A new lion is coming from Africa!'

'I wonder what Leo thinks of it,' remarked her sister, Louisa.

'I don't know' mused Pippa. 'They'll probably keep them in separate cages to prevent them from fighting.'

'Well, I think it's about time we had some new blood around here!' commented Amy.

The great day arrived and so did the lion. David Attenborough was there with two camera crews – one to film the lion and the other to film the cameramen filming the lion. A crowd of eager visitors gathered in front of the empty cage as a large crate was rolled along on a trolley via the enclosure, through a gated tunnel and into the cage. The head of the lion house removed the bolt that was keeping the door in place and stepped back nimbly into the tunnel, closing the barred gate behind him. A hush fell upon the spectators gathered around the outside bars, waiting for their first glimpse of the newcomer.

The lion sat for a few moments assessing the situation. It was cold and the light was grey. Straw was scattered on the cement floor in front of him; to his right he could see a crowd of people straining their necks for a look at him, talking in hushed voices; a large camera with a zoom lens was poking through the outer set of bars.

'I'll soon have that!' he thought to himself.

But most disconcertingly. there was a large lion with a fluffy mane only three yards in front of him! He growled and the other lion growled back, revealing a full set of teeth. Cautiously the new lion placed a paw outside the crate.

'Here he comes!' crooned David Attenborough and a thrill of anticipation electrified the crowd.

The neighbouring lion clawed at him through the bars, but the young lion soon realized that they prevented him from coming any nearer.

'Well, he's not much of a threat,' thought the older lion, observing the scruffy creature before him. 'He's thin and mangy and his mane is all dishevelled.'

The two lions sat and roared at each other for a while, until the younger lion became tired. To the disappointment of the crowd, he got back into his crate, lay down and fell asleep.

After about an hour, his dreams of the Serengeti were disturbed by a familiar smell. He opened his eyes to see a keeper thrusting a large chunk of raw meat through the double bars with a pitch fork. He couldn't tell what animal it was, but he was hungry, so he settled down to his first meal in his new home. His neighbour also had something to eat, so he didn't have to fight over it. They both devoured their dinner, after which they started grooming themselves. When they had finished, they both lay back, eyeing each other, not without curiosity.

'So,' remarked the incumbent, 'you must be the new lion they are all talking about!'

'So it would seem!' replied the newcomer.

'Do lions have names in Africa?' enquired Leo, swatting a fly from his nose.

'They do. I'm called Marlon because I'm the Wild One.'

The other lion regarded him in silence.

'And what should I call you?' asked Marlon.

'My name is Leonardo, like Leonardo di Caprio, but everyone calls me Leo.'

'How did you come to be here?' enquired Marlon. 'Were you born in captivity?'

'No,' he sighed, 'I too was born in the wild, but my mother was shot by poachers, so my two sisters and I were captured and brought over here.'

He paused, blinking back the tears that had welled up unbidden in his eyes. 'What about you?'

'One day I was walking across the plain, minding my own business, when a group of men in a jeep approached me,' explained Marlon. 'I thought they were too far away to harm me, but one of them pointed a stick at me. I felt something sharp in my flank. I began to feel drowsy so I lay down, and within a few minutes I was asleep. The next thing I knew I was being jostled along in a crate, heading for the airport.'

'What's an airport?' asked Leo.

'Oh, it's a horrible place where they keep planes. They put you in the hold where it's dark and stuffy, and then the plane takes off. It makes a terrible noise and you feel the pull of the engine. It made me feel sick. After a while, it just bumps around in the sky until it is time to land, then it's the same thing again, only you're in a different place.'

During the pause that followed, Leo puzzled over the wonders of modern travel.

'So, is this it?' asked Marlon, looking around the cage. 'It seems like a prison cell.'

'The gate at the back leads to the enclosure which features a pool surrounded by rocks,' Leo replied. He omitted to tell Marlon about the lionesses.

'Do you hunt?' asked Marlon.

'I'm afraid there are no opportunities for hunting. Besides, there's no need. The keepers feed us twice a day.'

'What do you do all day? Don't you get bored?'

'Oh, I do a lot of pacing and snarling at the crowd,' replied Leo. 'Don't worry, you'll soon get used to it!'

The next day Marlon was allowed out into the enclosure. When he emerged from the tunnel, he stood still, surveying the scene before him. It was as Leo had described it, but much smaller than he had imagined, with a few bushes and trees for shade. The water in the pool was a clear blue, with not an alligator in sight.

The lionesses were sprawled around, feigning indifference to the new arrival.

'He's a bit scruffy!' remarked Amy, swatting a fly from her nose.

'Look how skinny he is!' exclaimed Zelda. 'You can see his ribs!'

'I suppose they don't get regular meals in Africa, the way we do here!' yawned Pippa.

'And look at all those battle scars!' exclaimed Amy.

'I quite like them.' remarked Louisa, pausing in her toilette. 'It shows he's not a sissy!'

After a week or so he began to put on weight. The females started to warm to his Devil-may-care attitude; Louisa even offered to groom his mane.

Leo continued to be jealous of him, but because they were not allowed out of their cages at the same time, the longed-for confrontation never took place. Besides, Leo began to enjoy their conversations, which relieved the monotony. Leo was able to exhibit his superior knowledge of life at the zoo, while secretly he was fascinated by Marlon's tales of the Serengeti.

Eventually the time came for Marlon's return to his homeland. He looked back at the months he had spent in the zoo, and knew he would miss the lionesses and the regular meals but he couldn't wait to get back to the open plains. Again, he was darted and hauled into a crate, which was driven off in a lorry to the airport. The only difference this time was that Leo came with him in a separate crate.

When they touched down in Africa, he could feel the difference immediately. The air was warm and humid and it smelled dusty. After a 12-hour trip along a bumpy road, they finally arrived at an animal sanctuary close to Marlon's old home.

The keepers at the shelter provided them with chunks of meat and bowls of fresh water, and left them for the night to recover from their exhausting journey.

The next morning, they were transferred into smaller cages and wheeled onto the back of an open truck. David Attenborough and his crews followed in a jeep.

Marlon's heart swelled with joy as they passed through familiar territory, his mane flowing in the breeze. Home at last!

Finally, they stopped on the brow of a hill and the two lions stood surveying the scene in wonder from behind bars. A riverbed sprawled before them on the reddish-brown soil. Everywhere you could see herds of animals who had come to the river to quench their thirst – zebras, wildebeests, springboks, hyenas, wild dogs, baboons, elephants and giraffes. Hippopotamuses wallowed in the mud, glaring at the intruders, and alligators languished at eye-level, hoping for a snack, while vultures circled above.

'Wow!' exclaimed Leo. 'It's so vast – and there are so many animals!'

He couldn't fail to be impressed.

A worker from the sanctuary had placed some chunks of meat near the jeep. The captives were released from their cages, and immediately they fell upon the food.

'They do this so that we stay close to the jeep,' remarked Marlon between mouthfuls.

After they had finished, they looked around. There was nothing preventing them from leaving.

'Come on! I'll show you around,' offered Leo's guide, heading towards the river bed.

Leo followed him as fast as he could, allowing for the fact that he had not had time to digest his breakfast. The younger lion came to a stop behind some bushes that ran along by the river.

'Do you see those hippopotamuses along the shore?' whispered Marlon as soon as Leo had caught up with him. 'Be careful. You should never come between a hippopotamus and water.'

'Why not?' asked Leo.

'They don't like it – and they can be dangerous!' replied Marlon. 'And another thing – can you see those scruffy-looking dogs?'

'Yes,' answered Leo, squinting in the bright sunlight.

'They are hyenas. Stay away from them. They are our natural enemies,' pronounced Marlon.

'But what harm can they do? They are smaller than us!'

'They can gang up on us and surround us!'

After a pause, Marlon spotted a young zebra on the fringe of the herd. It was too big to be under the protection of its mother, and yet smaller than a full-grown animal.

'Come on,' urged Marlon. 'Let's do some hunting!'

The young cat started out moving slowly through the long grass. Leo followed him close behind. As they stepped out into the open area, one of the herd spotted him and let out a cry that sent the rest of the animals fleeing for safety. Startled, the young zebra looked up from his grazing and followed the rest of the herd, but he lagged behind. Marlon put on a spurt and soon caught up with him. The terrified animal tried to escape, zig-zagging and running in circles in an effort to avoid the lion's claws, but to no avail. Marlon jumped up and clawed at his hind quarters in an attempt to bring him down, but the zebra, though badly scratched, managed to wriggle away. After two or three attempts by the lion, the zebra escaped and ran off to join the other animals.

Marlon was miffed. He must be losing his touch! But it was hard hunting alone. He turned round to look for Leo, but he was nowhere to be seen. Limping slightly, he retraced his steps until he found his companion sitting down, gasping for breath.

'What happened to you?' asked Marlon. 'I could have brought him down if you had been there!'

'I'm sorry!' gasped Leo. 'I couldn't keep up! I'm not used to all this exercise!'

To make things worse, the jeep had been following them at a distance and the cameramen had filmed Marlon's embarrassing failure.

At the end of the day, they returned hungry to the vehicle, where they received a free dinner.

Each morning the two lions set off early after breakfast to hunt. At first Leo found it impossible to keep up with Marlon, but as the weeks passed his stamina and speed improved. One day Marlon spotted a young wildebeest at the edge of a herd. He soon isolated him and drove him down towards the river. The wildebeest, caught between the alligator-infested water and a lion in full chase, ran along the dried-up part of the river bed. A steep bank to his right prevented him from changing direction. As the river curved to the right, swallowing up the dry ground, the wildebeest found himself trapped. The cornered animal turned around and faced his pursuer, revealing his tusks in a desperate attempt to intimidate him. Leo, who had been following the chase along the river bank, was now positioned directly above their prey. With one leap he floated through the air, and before the wildebeest realized he was being attacked from above, landed on the small creature with the full weight of his body.

'Well done, Leo!' remarked Marlon.

Leo was overjoyed with his first catch. They settled down to their meal before other predators had time to close in on them. The two lions returned to the jeep that evening, but to tell the truth, they hardly had the appetite for dinner.

Once Leo had regained his strength and they had learned to work as a team, they found it easy to hunt together.

One day Marlon said to Leo, 'You know what day tomorrow is?'

'My birthday?'

Marlon could never tell if he was joking.

'Not as far as I know,' he replied. 'It's the day you have to return to London. What are you going to do? Are you going to return to your cold grey prison cell with regular meals, or are you going to stay here and hunt with me?'

'What about my sisters – and the other lionesses?' he asked, thinking wistfully of Amy.

'They are safe and well-fed. Besides, we may be able to join another pride, or meet a couple of stray females and start our own families.'

Leo brightened up at the thought.

'I'll stay here with you!'

'We don't need their handouts anymore!' remarked Marlon.

So that evening the lions failed to return for their dinner. The flaming disc of the sun sank behind the umbrella-shaped trees, throwing them into silhouette. In the cool of the evening, Leo settled down to his first night of real freedom, feeling both apprehensive and excited.

The next morning, the crew was in an uproar. Everyone was irritable because of Leo's defection. The second crew wanted to know who was going to film them filming the first crew filming the animals. In the end they decided that they would all film each other and forget about the wildlife. David Attenborough soon put a stop to the arguments. He set off in the jeep in an attempt to find the escapee, waving a piece of paper in the air and calling out, 'Leo, come back! What about your contract?'

But the two lions were far out of earshot, already making plans for their next hunting expedition.

First published in *The Market Place*
January 2020

The Pigeon and the Nightingale

Percy the Pigeon lived in a place called Essex, not far from the Thames Estuary. He was in love with a lady pigeon named Esmeralda, but she did not return his affections. He would strut about, puffing out his chest, but she would just look the other way or flutter off. In the end he was so desperate he went to see the Wise Old Owl who lived in an oak tree.

Ollie the Owl was a nocturnal bird, and didn't much care to be woken up in the middle of the day, but when he saw Percy's sad face, he softened his manner, flapping around until he found his glasses.

'There,' he said, 'that's better!'

To tell the truth, he didn't really need to wear glasses because he had excellent eyesight. As any field mouse might tell you, he could spot a rodent at twenty metres. But he had a reputation for being intelligent, so he had to maintain his image.

'So, young fellow, what's the problem?'

'It's Esmeralda. I'm in love with her, but she doesn't take any notice of me! What can I do?'

'So, what have you got?' asked the owl, who had recently taken advantage of a cheap flight to New York and had come back with an accent and an attitude.

'What have I got?' repeated the pigeon.

'Yes, how do you whoo her?'

'Well, I strut about and fluff up my chest and coo,' he explained.

'Let's hear you coo!'

Percy took a deep breath and pursed his beak: 'Coo! Coo!'

Ollie hooted with laughter.

'That's it?' he asked incredulously. 'Coo! Coo?'

'Well, what's wrong with it?' replied Percy defensively. 'That's how the other pigeons woo.'

'But you've got to offer more than the other birds. You've got to up your game and beat the competition!'

'Beat the competition? But how do I do that?'

'Maybe you should take some singing lessons,' suggested the owl.

'But who would be able to teach me to sing?' asked Percy.

Ollie adjusted his glasses, which gave him time to think.

'Let me see now ...'

He fluffed up his feathers and moved back and forth sideways along the branch.

'I've got it!' he exclaimed, coming to a stop and waving a wing in the air. 'How about a nightingale?'

'And where would I find a nightingale?' enquired Percy, who wasn't even sure what a nightingale was.

'Well, there aren't many left,' replied the owl. 'They're an Endangered Species.'

'What's an Endangered Species?' asked Percy.

Ollie made a gesture with his wing, as if cutting his own throat.

'They used to live in the woods but man has destroyed their habitat so most of them have disappeared.'

Percy thanked him and set off on his quest.

He followed the river towards the setting sun. Soon he found himself flying over miles and miles of suburbs – houses with small gardens, roads, shops and railway stations. As he reached the centre of the city, he could see all the large buildings – church spires and towers, office blocks and high-rise flats so tall they blocked out the sun. Then he recognized Nelson's Column in Trafalgar Square. He had heard about it because he had a cousin called Bertram who lived there. Perhaps he could pay him a visit. But there were hundreds of birds flocking around and the traffic was so noisy he couldn't even hear himself think, so he carried on flying. As the sun went down, he came to rest in a green park. Settling on a high branch, out of reach from predators, he fell asleep, exhausted from his journey.

The next morning at dawn he was awoken by a chorus of birdsong. He had overslept! He asked around but none of the birds had seen a nightingale. Some of them didn't even know of their existence. So after stuffing himself with some peanuts he had found lying on the ground, Percy set off again, following the River Thames to its source. He recognized Oxford from descriptions he had heard about its spires and domes, but soon the river became narrow, and further on it dried up.

Percy took a turn south towards the sea, stopping to rest when he reached the coast. Every time he came to a new place, he would ask around about nightingales but no-one could help him. So his search went on. Days turned into weeks. The pink petals fell off the trees as the warm summer days arrived. Sometimes it would rain, and he had to find shelter under the leaves of a tree or on a ledge. Most of the time he felt sad and lonely, missing his friends and family and wondering about Esmeralda.

Summer turned to Autumn as green leaves changed to red and gold.

Sometimes he would wake up to a frost upon the ground, and he knew that winter would soon be here.

He was feeling dejected and wondering if he should give up his search, when he spied a crow pulling up a worm from the furrows of a ploughed field. When the crow saw him, he let go of one end of his breakfast, which swiftly slid back into the safety of the damp earth.

'Caw!' he said, noticing that Percy was down in the beak. 'What's the matter with you?'

'I've travelled far and wide looking for a nightingale, but no-one can help me find one.'

'What do you need a nightingale for?' asked the crow, whose name was Cuthbert.

'I'm in love with Esmeralda, but she doesn't even know I exist. I thought if I could learn to sing like a nightingale, she might show an interest in me.'

'Well there used to be a few that lived in the wood near Miller's Creek, but the humans chopped it down and built a shopping mall. Most of them disappeared, but there might be one or two left down by the coppice.'

Percy's eyes shone with hope.

'Thank you, Cuthbert. I can't tell you how grateful I am!'

And with a flutter of his wings, he set off for the spinney.

He settled on a log but could hear nothing unusual, apart from the dormice snoring, the badgers complaining about the damp weather and a couple of squirrels fighting over a stash of hazelnuts.

As dusk was casting its grey shadows over the trees, he began to feel depressed again because he had failed to locate a nightingale. Then he remembered what the owl had told him – that they were nocturnal, which meant they only sang during the night or at daybreak.

He found himself a comfortable branch and soon nodded off. But every time he heard an unusual sound he would wake up with a start.

The air grew chill as a new moon rose over the bare branches of the trees.

Then he heard it. The most beautiful birdsong in the world! Its trills and arpeggios were spellbinding. The voice rose in a crescendo, adding one ornament after another. Percy sat entranced. Without wanting to disturb the singer, he hopped and fluttered from branch to branch until he could see him; a small brown bird perched on a twig, half-hidden by a screen of dying leaves. At first, it was hard to believe that such a plain little creature could produce such a wonderful rich sound. Then he stretched his neck and opened his beak again, and musical notes poured out like honey. After a while of this virtuoso performance, the nightingale paused for a rest. Percy approached him shyly.

'That was wonderful! I have never heard such a beautiful song before in all my life!'

After the little bird had recovered from the surprise of having a secret admirer, he replied, 'Well thank you, young friend. My name's Nigel the Nightingale. And your name is?'

'Percy, Percy the Pigeon.'

'And is there something I can do for you?'

'Yes! Could you teach me to sing? You see, I'm in love with a pigeon called Esmeralda, but she's not interested in me. I thought that if I could learn to sing like you, she might change her mind.'

'Well, it would depend on your vocal range and your natural ability. Let's hear what you sound like.'

Percy drew a deep breath, puffed up his chest and let out a 'Coo! Coo!'

Nigel looked at him in astonishment.

'Well, it might take a while,' he commented. 'The question is, what's in it for me?'

'What's in it for you?' asked Percy. 'What do you mean?'

'Well, if I'm going to spend my valuable time teaching you to sing instead of migrating to warmer climes, I would need some kind of recompense.'

The pigeon shuffled awkwardly from one scaly foot to the other, not knowing what to say. After a minute's silence he came up with an idea.

'I could teach you how to coo!' he offered.

Nigel stared at him open-beaked. Then he suddenly burst out laughing. Have you ever heard a nightingale laugh? It sounds like tinkling bells on a frosty night. Reaching out his tiny wing, he slapped Percy on his broad back.

'I like a bird with a sense of humour!' he exclaimed.

Percy didn't know what a sense of humour was, but he was glad that he had one, if that was what it took to make the nightingale teach him.

So from that night forth, Nigel took Percy under his wing.

They found a cosy little bole in an oak tree. During the day, Percy would forage for food between naps, but at night he would practice scales and learn trills. At first he found it difficult adjusting to the new regime, but as the weeks wore on he became used to it.

Then one night in the middle of winter, when icy winds whistled through the bare branches and the snow fell softly on the forest floor, Nigel made an announcement:

'That's it! You've had enough lessons and it's time I headed south. I should have left months ago!'

Percy was sad to see him go, but he thanked him for all his help, and waved his wing as Nigel disappeared into the rising sun.

The pigeon realized it was time for him to leave too, so he set off towards home.

The terrain looked totally different under snow, but he kept the sea to his right so he wouldn't get lost. At night he would rest on a branch or inside a hollow log, but he would never go to sleep or wake up without practicing all that Nigel had taught him. He drew curious looks from the other birds and animals that lived nearby, some of whom crowded around to listen to his performance, but he was proud of his achievement.

Percy finally reached home as the snow melted and the daffodils bloomed. He found a convenient branch, drew in a deep breath and began his first song. Within minutes the other birds appeared. Then he saw Esmeralda! She was as beautiful as ever. His heart pounded but he carried on singing. The woods echoed with the sound of his voice, which was like a waterfall cascading over rocks. He added trills, ornaments and arpeggios and even threw in some staccato and a diminished seventh. When he had finished he looked over at her to see her response.

'What on earth was that?' she asked. 'You go off for a year and when you come back, you don't even sound like a pigeon!'

With a sniff, she flew off. Percy was devastated.

Then he noticed a younger pigeon peering at him from behind the fresh green foliage. It was Beryl. She was only a fledgling when he had left, but her spiky fluff had now been replaced by a shiny new coat of feathers.

Beryl edged towards him shyly.

'That was the most beautiful sound I have ever heard!' she lisped.

'Oh, do you think so?' asked Percy, puffing out his chest.

First published in *The Market Place*
December 2019

Love on a Bus

A Traveller's Tail

I first visited Arundel as a teenager, while on a walking holiday with a friend. I still have a vision of ambling along a pavement dappled by the afternoon sun shining through tall trees as the rounded towers of a fairy-tale castle rose up above us, dreamlike in the sunbeams. But that was many years ago.

Last year I found myself staying in the area once more just 6 miles from Arundel. With free time on my hands, I thought I might awaken some happy memories of my youth. Being unsure of the bus timetable, I took a taxi. The drive gave me ample time to admire the South Downs, rising like a green shoulder to my left. When I eventually arrived in Arundel, I got out of the car. The town was far enough inland for the sea breeze to have died down. It was a perfect spring morning. I found the village to be small, charming and unspoilt. Meandering past tea shops, restaurants and purveyors of antiques, I arrived at the castle walls.

On my previous visit, we had not gone inside the castle, probably because it was late in the day. Another possibility was that we did not have enough money for the entrance fee. Or perhaps I was afraid of breaking the magic spell.

This time I could afford the price of a ticket.

I wandered from room to room, marvelling at the weaponry and suits of armour. As I peered out of the arrow slits onto the surrounding grassy area, I tried to imagine Henry I's men besieging the fortress in an effort to claw back power from the barons and earls. The higher I climbed, the narrower the spiral staircase became, until there was insufficient room for an attacker to wield a sword. Those defending the castle were armed with small knives and daggers, which put them at an advantage. Unfortunately for them, it was not enough to prevent Henry from taking possession of his castle.

When I had had my fill of portcullises, I wandered out through the green peace of the gardens to the main gate towards the bus stop. On cue, a double-decker country bus trundled around the corner. I sat in the front seat where I could see the passengers as they mounted the step.

At the next stop, a woman got on followed by a large dog. I think he was a poodle, but not one of those dinky toy kinds with Mme. Pompadour haircuts and pink ribbons. This one was a Proper Dog, with reddish, salt and pepper fur left long enough to reveal its natural wave. His owner was brandishing a leash, unattached to the dog. An elderly couple rushed over to him and started petting him, but as soon as he saw me, he came over and sat on the floor by my side. His head was on the same level as mine, and we both sat facing the other passengers as they got on. Those already on the bus laughed.

I stroked the top of his head and his ears.

'What's his name?' I asked.

'Pippin,' replied the owner, 'like the apple.'

She paused, waving the lead about.

'I suppose I should really put him on his leash.'

She called to Pippin but the dog ignored her. The woman started to get embarrassed; she must have regretted the money she had wasted on dog obedience school. The more flustered she got, the more the other commuters laughed. Pippin stayed calmly in his chosen place by my side.

At the next stop, more passengers got on the bus. When they saw Pippin sitting next to me, they let out an 'Oooh!' of delight and laughed. Those already on the bus laughed even louder, being in on the joke.

'How old is he?' I asked his mistress, but the woman pretended to be busy with something in her bag.

I asked her again in a louder voice this time, but she continued to ignore my question. I sensed a touch of jealousy, and decided not to push the point.

As we drew close to my destination, I began to wonder what would happen if I got off the bus first. Would Pippin try to follow me? Would there be a custody battle? Or if his owner got off before me, would

Pippin refuse to move from my side? Would an unseemly tussle ensue as the passengers cheered us on and the bus driver grumbled?

We arrived in Littlehampton, and as it happened, all three of us got off at the same stop. Pippin trotted along at his owner's side without so much as a backward glance. I followed at a short distance, hoping for a turn of the head, one last lingering look filled with longing from those fudge-brown eyes, a whimper of regret or a woof of apology. But he continued looking straight in front of him, his head held high, our brief encounter forgotten as he visualized the contents of the bowl that awaited him under the kitchen table.

Frailty, thy name is Pippin!*

* In Shakespeare's play, Hamlet addresses his mother with the words: 'Frailty, thy name is woman!'

The Great Escape

It is a little-known fact that a group of cats was employed by British Intelligence during World War II to spy on the Enemy in German-occupied France. Their mission was to infiltrate German forces and relay valuable information to the French Resistance.

Such a unit was the 3rd Essex Battalion, code name 'Feisty Felines.'

* * *

It was past midnight as the small plane circled above farmland in Northern France amidst thunder crashing and flashes of lightening. The moon and stars had been obliterated by heavy storm clouds, making visibility almost zero.

'We've reached the given co-ordinates, Sir!' the pilot called from the cockpit. Monty, a ginger and white cat in a combat jacket, looked out of the window, but could see nothing but rain as it streamed down the sides of the plane.

'A-OK, Raffles,' he called back. 'Can you see any landmarks?'

'Only a dim light directly below us.'

Monty slid open the side door. A blast of wind knocked him back, and the rain pelted in. He peeped over the edge into the black void. There below him he could make out a small light, flickering like a faint hope.

'O.K. boys,' he called. 'Prepare to jump!'

The cats adjusted the straps of their parachutes and lined up in front of the gaping hole.

'Tiger! Jump!'

A sinuous ginger tabby moved towards the open door, quivered for a moment on the threshold, then leaped into the void.

'Good luck, Tiger,' he called, but his voice was all but drowned by a clap of thunder.

'Sooty!'

'Yes, sir!'

'Jump!'

'Cheeky and Squeaky! Jump!'

The twins insisted upon jumping together, so that they could hold paws. Monty worried in case their parachutes might become entangled, but they always seemed to manage.

Finally, the only other cat left on board was Tommy, Monty's Second-in-Command.

'See you soon. Have a safe jump!'

As Tommy's black tail disappeared through the gaping doorway, Monty turned to the pilot.

'Thank you, Raffles. *Bon Voyage!*'

'Good luck, sir!' he replied, but his words were lost to Monty as he took the plunge into the unknown.

Raffles spoke into the microphone over the crackles and squeaks: 'Mission accomplished.'

Turning the plane around, he headed back towards the English Channel.

* * *

Monty fell helter-skelter into what felt like a black hole as the wind and rain buffeted him about. His heart racing, he fumbled for the toggle on his parachute, which, to his relief, opened out above him like an umbrella and slowed down his fall. He came to land in what appeared to be a large meadow. He looked around but couldn't see much except a dim light from a lantern, about 50 metres away. Then he heard Charley's voice nearby.

'Help! Help! My parachute's caught in a tree!'

Monty made his way towards his plaintive cries. He could just make out Charley's plump form dangling from the branch of a tree at the edge of the field.

'Hold on, Charley. I'm coming!'

Within seconds Monty had climbed the tree and had removed a penknife from one of his many pockets. He cut the cords of Charley's parachute one by one, until he came to the fourth and last one.

'Prepare to drop!' he called above the noise of the thunder and rain.

He heard a 'plop' and ran down to the base of the tree trunk, where Charley stood on all fours, rain dripping from his fur.

'Are you all right" asked Monty.

'As right as rain!' he grinned.

They made their way towards the glimmering light, where they found the other cats gathered around a Siamese wearing a beret and holding a lantern.

He approached the Siamese.

'My name's Monty, the Commanding Officer of Special Operations. Thank you for guiding us here!'

'I'm Lulu, ze Chief Co-ordinator of Volunteers. Sank you for coming to 'elp us!'

Monty glanced swiftly around the group.

'Is everyone here?' he asked.

'All present and correct, suh!' replied Tommy, 'except for Mickey, who has twisted his ankle.'

Monty turned to Mickey.

'Are you OK? Can you walk?'

'I can manage,' was his reply.

'How many of you are there?' asked Lulu.

'Twelve altogether,' he replied.

'Come, let's get out of ze rain. Follow me.'

Lulu set off followed by the bedraggled bunch to a two-storey farmhouse. A faint glow came from one of the downstairs windows.

Lulu turned round and addressed them in a hushed voice: 'You must be quiet! Ze farmer and 'is wife are upstairs asleep!'

She jumped through a half-open window. The rest followed her, glad to be out of the drenching rain. They found themselves in a spacious kitchen with a hearth at one end. The dying embers sent out a warm glow and shed light on their surroundings.

Lulu went to the larder and brought out a large jug of milk. The other cats pulled out their tin cans from their rucksacks and held them out as she poured milk into them.

'Mmmmm! Fresh milk!' purred Sooty.

'I'm sorry I 'ave nothing else to give you,' whispered Lulu. 'Ze Germans, zey have taken everysing – ze chickens, ze pigs. We are lucky zey left us a few cows!'

'Don't apologize!' replied Monty. 'The milk is very welcome.'

When they had finished drinking, they sat around the remains of the fire and dried out their fur.

A grey Persian called Blue, who was in charge of navigation, pulled out a folded map, which he studied by the light of the glowing embers.

'Where are you 'eading?' asked Lulu, looking over his shoulder at the map.

'Pijon,' he replied, checking with his compass.

'That's about 15 kilometres from 'ere,' she said. 'You turn right at the gate and follow ze road.'

'Thank you for all you help,' replied Monty, pulling a cap from his rucksack and pulling it over one ear.

'Well, I think we had better be going. We've a long way ahead of us and we want to get there before dawn.'

The other cats were hoping to stay in the warm kitchen out of the rain, but they knew they had a mission to accomplish. They all thanked Lulu and saluted her as they followed Monty out of the window one by one.

'*Au revoir!*' she called as she watched them go through the torrential rain down the garden path leading to the gate.

* * *

The worst of the storm had passed, but they still had to make their way under a heavy downpour. Dry fur was not an option. They trudged on regardless of the weather conditions, with Mickey lagging behind.

At daybreak they reached the outskirts of a small village.

'Is this it?' asked Monty.

Blue consulted his map.

'This is it!' he confirmed.

They came to a halt outside a row of terraced houses set in farmland. On the ground floor, holes gaped where windows had once been, the garden was overgrown and altogether the building had a sad, abandoned look.

'They're probably farm labourer's cottages,' Tommy mused.

Monty jumped over the crumbling stone wall and the other cats followed one by one so as not to look conspicuous. He stretched up on his front paws and peered through one of the broken windows.

'This will do!' he announced and hopped over the window sill.

Glad to be out of the rain, the other cats followed suit.

Once inside, they surveyed their new home. Stone slabs covered the floor and in the centre of the room was a large wooden table surrounded by six chairs, two of which had been toppled.

'It looks as if the family left in a hurry!' commented Monty.

A fireplace stood to the right with a pile of logs beside it. A large black pot hung from a tripod in the middle of the hearth. Worn armchairs stood on either side.

At a word from Monty, Cheeky and Squeaky started clearing away the ashes and arranging branches and twigs in a pyramid.

Soon the cats were gathered in front of a roaring fire. First they dried their fur and adjusted their whiskers.

Mimi, a white long-haired Persian, was particularly upset at having wet fur. He combed it and arranged it as well as he could, all the time whining about the snags and knots in it.

To the left of the hearth stood a wood-burning stove where the previous occupants had done some of their cooking; china was ranged on a dresser and pots and pans stood on the shelves along the back wall.

Monty pushed open the larder door and started taking stock of the left-over food. The butter was rancid and the milk sour. Only the hard crust of a loaf of bread remained, surrounded by dry crumbs. The mice fled at the sight of the ginger tabby.

Sooty, a black short-hair with white paws and bib, called out from the top shelf: 'Look, Sir! They've left some tins!'

He passed them down to Monty, who inspected them, turning them over in his paws.

'Judging by the picture, they contain fish!'

'Fish!' exclaimed the other cats.

They were tired and hungry, and hadn't had a proper meal since their paws had left English soil.

'Here, Mimi!' called Monty, 'Can you try your paw at opening this?'

'Why does everybody call me Mimi?' he complained pettishly, 'My real name's Arthur?'

'Yes, but that's your code name!' replied Monty.

Although Mimi was snooty and a bit of a whiner, he was an expert with Gadgets, and could pick a lock at ten yards. Mimi examined the can.

'Do you need a tin-opener?' offered Sooty. 'There's one here!'

Sooty had discovered the cutlery drawer.

'Tin opener!' Mimi sniffed.

He had noticed a key at one end of the can which he turned. Slowly but surely, he eased back the lid to reveal a row of sardines in tomato sauce. The other cats crowded round in excitement as the smell rose to their quivering nostrils.

'Pass me the rest,' he called to Sooty. Soon five tins of sardines were lying opened in a row on the table.

'Enough for a feast!' exclaimed Charley, a chubby black cat who acted as Quartermaster and Cook.

Each cat had already taken down a plate from the dresser and was waiting eagerly in line as Charley banged a saucepan with a metal spoon. Tiger and Patch, who had been exploring upstairs, came rushing down to take their place in the queue. Charley doled out the sardines so that everyone got his share.

When they had licked their plates clean and were stretched in front of the fire washing themselves, Tommy remarked, 'There's a carpet under the table!'

All the cats turned to look, and indeed, what he said was true.

'That's a strange place for a carpet,' remarked Tommy. 'Why isn't it in front of the hearth?'

The twins looked at each other and then rushed over to the carpet and moved it out of the way.

'A trap door!' exclaimed Monty.

With some difficulty Cheeky slid the bolt and the two of them managed to lift up the door by hooking their claws into a brass ring.

They all crowded round and peered into the dark cellar. Monty led the way down the stone steps.

'Ugh! There's dust and cobwebs everywhere!' remarked Mimi, brushing down his coat.

Once their eyes had adjusted to the dark they realized that the vault ran the length of the four cottages. Rows of wooden shelves containing dusty bottles lined the stone walls.

'It's a wine cellar!' declared Peter, a delicate tabby with white markings, who was a bit of a connoisseur.

'Shall we bring the bottles upstairs?' asked Charley, who was fond of a tipple.

'Just one bottle!' replied Monty. 'That will be enough for now!'

They emerged from the cellar, Charley clutching the bottle under his arm.

Once back in the kitchen, Charley poured a small amount of the red liquid into the glasses that the other cats had lined up on the table. The wine glowed in the firelight as they raised their glasses.

'To the Feisty Felines!' called Monty.

'Success to our mission!' replied Peter, who was used to making toasts.

'By the way,' enquired Monty, turning to Tiger and Patch, 'what did you find upstairs?'

'Two bedrooms and a bathroom,' reported Tiger. 'In one bedroom there are two narrow beds ... '

' … and in the room above the kitchen a large bed and a wooden cot,' cut in Patch, 'and a fireplace. Oh, I nearly forgot, and a chest containing blankets, shawls and baby clothes.'

'Baby clothes?' asked Monty.

'Yes, little lacy things. Dresses and nightdresses and bonnets.'

'Why didn't the family take the clothes with them?' asked Mickey.

'They probably didn't have time,' replied Monty. 'What condition are the windows in?'

'There's glass in them,' replied Cheeky.

'Good! Then we'll sleep up there, away from the rain and wind. Douse the fire, Squeaky. We don't want anyone seeing the smoke.'

Reluctantly the twins sprinkled water on the burning logs until all that was left were smouldering embers.

They all made their way upstairs except Patch, an expert in unarmed combat, who had been assigned to guard duty. He longed to go to sleep and kept dozing off in stops and starts. He could imagine the other cats making themselves comfortable on the beds with the blankets and woollen shawls.

* * *

A cockerel crowed from a neighbouring farm, announcing the dawn of a new day. Patch woke up with a start. The rain had stopped and the sun rose over the window sill against a pale blue sky.

'Oh no!' he thought. 'I've slept all night! I'll be court-martialled if anyone finds out! I'd better check to see that everything is all right.'

He could hear strange voices speaking gruffly close by. Running to a front window and reaching up, he peeked out. To his horror the house was surrounded by dogs!

He ran upstairs two at a time. The rest of the cats were fast asleep sprawled over the beds, unaware of the danger they were in.

He approached Monty, tapping him gently with his paw.

'Sir! Wake up! We're surrounded! We've been betrayed!'

Monty jumped off the bed and ran towards the bedroom window. The garden was choc-a-bloc with dogs: a bloodhound with a monocle in his eye wearing a peeked cap, a bulldog, a German shepherd, a poodle, a rottweiler, a Jack Russell, a dachshund, a boxer, and a chihuahua. He didn't recognize the other breeds. All of them wore well-cut green belted jackets. From their belts hung holsters and in each holster was a gun.

When the dogs saw Monty's face at the window, they all started barking and howling.

The cats ran across the landing to a window that overlooked the back garden. To their horror the yard was also filled with dogs yelping and generally kicking up a racket.

'We're trapped!' exclaimed Mimi. 'What are we going to do?'

'We're outnumbered and the dogs are all armed,' remarked Monty. 'There's only one thing we can do.'

'What's that?' asked Cheeky.

'Make friends with them!' came the reply.

'Make friends with the Germans?' exclaimed Tommy. 'That's treason!'

Monty turned to Charley.

'Fetch me a white handkerchief or towel from the chest!'

He came back with a long white baby's gown.

'This is all I could find,' explained Charley apologetically.

'That will do fine,' replied Monty, taking a stick from the pile of logs and slipping it through the sleeves.

'Open the window!'

With a heave from the twins, the window creaked opened and Monty leaned out, brandishing the makeshift flag.

The bloodhound chortled.

'So you surrender!' he declared. 'Very wise.'

'Yes,' replied Monty, 'we surrender under the rules of the Geneva Convention!'

'Of course, under the Geneva Convention. What do you think we are? Animals?'

The bloodhound started guffawing at his own joke. He laughed so hard he nearly choked.

'Come downstairs and through the front door one at a time with your paws in the air!' he commanded once he had recovered his composure.

Monty dropped back into the bedroom and the twins shut the window.

'Charley, Tommy, put the shawls and blankets back in the chest! The rest follow me!'

Monty walked downstairs carrying the banner and opened the front door. He stepped out into the garden into a semi-circle of yapping dogs.

'Silence!' barked the bloodhound. Turning towards Monty, he asked, 'Are you the officer in charge?'

'I am Lieutenant Commander Monty of the Third Essex Platoon!' he announced proudly, saluting.

'I am Herr Komandant Bosch. You may address me as 'Herr Komandant' or 'Sir.' How many are in your unit?'

'Twelve altogether, including myself.'

'Sir!' the Herr Komandant reminded him sharply.

'Sir!' replied Monty, saluting again for good measure.

By this time all the cats had followed him out into the garden and were standing with their paws in the air.

Bosch gave the order for the cats to be searched by three of the dogs, while another six went inside the house to look around the premises.

When the dogs had finished their search, the bloodhound told them to stand at ease. He walked around the rows, asking each cat for his name, which the poodle wrote down on a notepad. The dogs exploring the house came out and reported on what they had found – nothing much except a few pieces of furniture.

'Any food?' asked the bloodhound.

'Only some stale crumbs of bread, sour milk and mouldy cheese – oh and some empty sardine cans,' replied the German shepherd.

The Komandant ordered the cats back inside, where they were told to stay.

'There will be dogs on sentry duty in the garden at all times, so don't try to escape!' he barked.

They filed back into the house and closed the door. Outside the German shepherd and a Yorkshire terrier were left to keep an eye on them. The Alsatian paced back and forth outside the window, every now and then looking inside to see what the cats were doing.

Monty ran upstairs and motioned for the other cats to follow him. As they passed the windows in the rear overlooking the back garden, they could see another two dogs on sentry duty. In the adjacent cottage they could hear the sound of the other dogs moving about in the next room.

Mickey pressed his ear against the wall.

'What are they saying?' whispered Monty.

'He says that he has contacted Headquarters and is waiting for instructions … someone is saying we shall probably try to escape … by digging a tunnel into the garden! The other dogs are laughing.'

Monty sat down and took out his pipe, which he kept hidden in his cap, and sucked upon it. There was no tobacco in it and in reality, he didn't smoke. He had tried it once and nearly choked. But it helped him think and gave him an air of authority.

'Well, lads,' he said in a soft voice so that their neighbours could not hear them, 'any suggestions for an escape plan?'

'Perhaps we could climb up the chimney?' suggested Tommy.

They crowded round the bedroom fireplace and looked up the chimney. Tommy tried to climb up the side a couple of times, but he fell back, covered in soot.

'The sides are too smooth. It's difficult to get a pawhold!'

'Perhaps you could loosen some of the bricks and swivel them round, so that they can be used as footholds.'

'I'm not climbing up a chimney,' objected Mimi. 'I'll get my fur dirty!'

'That's all right,' replied Mickey. 'You can stay behind and explain to the Germans what happened!'

Monty peered up at the square of sky at the top.

'The passage is narrow. Some of us might find it hard to squeeze through,' he remarked.

Patch turned to Charley: 'You'd have to lose weight!'

'What about the noise,' asked Tiger.

'What we need is a Distraction,' announced Monty.

'What's a Distraction?' enquired Squeaky.

'We'll put on a concert for our German hosts. While we are rehearsing someone can tap away at the bricks!'

They all went down to the kitchen.

Tommy and Charley were assigned to brick duty. They found knives in the cutlery drawer

'Remember,' Monty warned them, 'wait until rehearsals begin and keep time to the music.'

'How about a hornpipe?' suggested Mickey, pulling out a tin whistle from his breast pocket. He climbed up on the table where Cheeky and Patch joined him, stamping and making as much noise as they could. The other cats clapped as they took their bow and jumped down.

'What about a choral work?' suggested Tommy. 'I think our friends would enjoy some Beethoven!'

Tommy and Tiger took down some pots and pans which they banged upon with metal spoons as the rest started meowing the melody of 'Ode to Joy.'

A few minutes later the front door banged open and the bloodhound walked in, carrying a cane under his arm. Everybody froze.

'What is the meaning of all this caterwauling? What a horrible din! It is giving me a headache!'

Monty stepped forward and saluted.

'We are sorry, Herr Komandant! We were rehearsing for a concert. We were going to invite you but we wanted it to be a surprise!'

'A concert you say? Well, you'll need a lot of rehearsing!'

'I do apologize. We're out of practice. We were going to offer you some light refreshment!'

'Light refreshment you say?' repeated the Komandant, adjusting his monocle. 'What do you mean?'

'Well, we found some wine that we wanted to share with you. It's a very good year!'

Monty picked up a bottle and offered it to the Komandant.

'Here, perhaps you'd like to sample some to see if it is to your liking?'

The bloodhound took the bottle and examined the label, but he couldn't read it because it was covered in dust and mildew.

'Well, I don't mind if I do!'

As he turned to go, he hesitated. 'And at what time will this err .. entertainment take place?'

'Tomorrow evening around 6 o'clock. Sir!' after which Monty saluted again.

The Komandant left, chuckling to himself.

* * *

The following afternoon the cats made their preparations for the concert. The kitchen table was covered with a lacy tablecloth that they had found in the chest and the polished glasses were lined up next to several bottles of red wine. Two bottles had been emptied except for a small amount of red liquid at the bottom. To this had been added water, which gave the bottle the appearance of containing rosé wine. Peter, who was to serve as wine waiter, had been instructed to give red wine to the dogs and rosé to the cats.

Promptly at six o'clock there was a knock at the front door. Monty opened it to reveal Herr Bosch.

'Come in, Sir, welcome to our little entertainment! Help yourself to a glass of wine!' Monty indicated the rows of filled glasses.

'Well, Danke schön!' he remarked, looking around the room. A fire crackled in the hearth and lit candles had been placed along the window sills.

'You've made it very cosy!' he remarked.

Monty indicated a chair to him.

'Please, make yourself comfortable!'

As the Komandant settled down, the rest of the dogs filed in and received their glass of red wine. Some sat on the few vacant chairs while others settled down on the floor in a semi-circle.

Mickey stepped centre-stage, pulled out a tin whistle from under his cap and placed it to his mouth. A hush fell over the expectant assembly.

Tapping his foot in time to the music he played the first few bars of a sailors' hornpipe. Three cats appeared from the open door leading into the hallway, dancing as they approached the stage, alternating their front paws in front and then behind them.

The dogs laughed and cheered, clapping their paws.

When the dancers reached the centre they placed their paws one above the other as if climbing an imaginary rope and danced around in a circle. Then they turned around on the spot, spinning their front paws around each other.

By now all the dogs were tapping their paws or slapping their thighs in time to the music.

The three cats then placed their paws on their hips and did a jig, facing the audience. They ended with a bow, while the dogs clapped and barked enthusiastically.

During the short interval that followed, Peter circulated with bottles of wine, topping up the dogs' empty glasses. They even passed glasses through the window to the Dalmatian and the other dogs who were on guard duty outside.

Next entered three cats dressed in long lace gowns and bonnets that they had found in the chest. They started singing 'Three little Maids from School,' and when one of the 'maids' winked at the Komandant, he laughed so much his monocle fell out and he nearly toppled off his chair.

In between each act, the wine waiter did his job, making sure that every dog had a full glass. A few tried to protest, but Peter could be very charming and persuasive.

'Why are you drinking rosé wine, while you serve us red?' the Komandant asked Monty.

'The rosé is of an inferior quality,' replied Monty. 'We couldn't possibly offer it to our guests.'

'How do I know this isn't spiked?' asked Herr Bosch, his monocle glinting.

'May I?' responded Monty, taking the half-empty glass from the Komandant's paw. After draining it in one gulp he called out to Peter, 'Another glass for the Komandant!'

The third performance was a solo given by Blue, who sang 'Danny Boy.' All the dogs wept at the plaintive melody and the touching lyrics. The Herr Komandant was positively blubbering, so much so that the bulldog, who was his Second-in-Command, had to lend him a handkerchief.

'It is not fitting for a German officer to cry,' he muttered through his clenched teeth.

For the finale, the cats grouped together on the stage for a choral version of 'Ode to Joy.' The dogs pricked up their ears eagerly as they heard the introductory notes, but when the cats started singing, it was obvious that some of them were flat, and that the harmonies weren't quite in key.

After about a minute of suffering, Herr Bosch stood up and announced in the middle of their rendition, 'Well, thank you very much. It has been a wonderful evening but we really have to be getting back!'

The other dogs stood up and followed him out the door. Some of them attempted a jig as they walked along the garden path. Through the paneless windows, the cats could hear strains of 'Three Little Maids from School.'

'That song about Danny – the words are so sad! First, he is hearing the pipes and he is going off to war, then he is coming back when the summer is on the meadow!' sobbed the Komandant. 'It reminds me of my poor little Mitzi waiting for me in Schlezwig-Holstein!'

The sounds of his weeping reached them as he walked along the garden path to his front door.

Another dog hiccupped.

The cats waited. After about 5 minutes a hush descended, followed by loud snoring.

'Blow out the candles and douse the fire!' whispered Monty.

Mimi checked the windows. 'The guards are all asleep, front and back!'

'Good! Let's go!'

They ran silently up the stone steps to the bedroom.

'Mission completed, Sir!' Tommy reported, raising his paw in a salute.

'Good lads!' he replied, leading the way to the fireplace. He poked his head up the chimney.

'Well done!' he commented as he saw the footholds that they had created.

'Tommy! Lead the way!'

He disappeared up the chimney breast. Out on the roof a full moon shone on an overgrown garden. Nothing stirred.

'The coast is clear!' he called back in a hoarse whisper.

One by one the others followed him.

Anyone who happened to be walking through the village after curfew that night would have witnessed an assortment of cats balancing along the apex of the roof in single file, silhouetted by the full moon, as they made their way to the far end. They slid down the roof to the gutter, where they climbed onto the outspread branches of a chestnut tree. When they reached the ground, they crossed the garden and climbed over the stone wall to freedom.

Thus, the Feisty Felines escaped from their canine captors and went on to complete their mission.

Because their actions came under the Official Secrets Act, no one could report their bravery or the contribution they made to the war effort by passing on information to the French Resistance. But many years have passed and their files have become declassified, so now their story may be told.

First published in *The Market Place*
March 2020

Bruno's Lament

Hannah stepped out onto the terrace and gazed at the hazy Mediterranean. It was hot and windless. The view didn't give her any relief from the heat. She wiped the perspiration from her forehead with the back of her arm. Of course, it was always hot on the Costa del Sol during the summer months. But this year had been worse than usual. They said it was because of global warming. There had even been a heatwave in the UK! She didn't think she could endure another summer like this. But where could she run to? She usually spent a couple of weeks in England with her daughter, but she always ended up babysitting Melanie's two small boys while their mother was at work. She adored them of course, but they were a bit of a handful, and she was always glad to come home. Besides, her daughter had already booked her up for the Easter holidays next year.

She really needed to go away to somewhere cool for July and August, but she couldn't afford to pay for a hotel, or even a self-catering flat for that length of time. Her meagre pension just about covered her living expenses. She had a small amount of money stashed away, but that was for emergencies like dental work.

Somewhere like Sweden might be nice. It would be cooler, but it would be light most of the time because of the long hours of daylight during the summer months.

But she didn't know anyone in Sweden, and she had heard it was very expensive.

Of course, she could always visit her son in Canada, but it was such a long way away. He worked in some research centre in Churchill, in the far north. The cost of the journey would be prohibitively expensive, and would take several days, but she hadn't seen him for 5 years, when he came on leave to Spain to visit her for 3 weeks. They had enjoyed their time together, but inevitably he needed to return to work. Once the idea of seeing Darren again had got into her head, she could think of nothing else. She went back into the villa and turned on the computer.

She started researching flights to Winnipeg, which was the nearest large city, and found one airline that cost around $1,000. That wasn't bad, except that she would have to change in Lisbon and Toronto. It would be a long haul, about 10 hours of flying time in all, but she could make a stop when she arrived in Canada. Of course she would have to pay for a hotel, but it would be worth it to break up the journey. The final leg, from Winnipeg to Churchill via Thomson, would cost about $2,000. Oh dear, she had already broken the bank, and that was only one way! But by now she was determined to visit her son. So she would spend all her savings. Who needs root canal anyway?

Of course, she would have to contact Darren before she got too carried away. She wrote him an e-mail, suggesting that she come and visit him. There was a

7-hour time difference, so it would be about 5 a.m. in Churchill; he was probably still in bed, fast asleep.

Three hours later she got his reply:

Dear Mum

It was great hearing from you and to know that you are thinking of coming to visit me in Churchill! You are very welcome, and can stay for as long as you like. It's quite pleasant in July and August, between 45°F and 65°F (7°C–16°C). You will only need to bring a couple of sweaters and a light jacket.

It's a small town of around 900 people, but there are some interesting things to do. As you know, it is the Polar Bear Capital of the World, so you could go on an organized tour and see them in their natural habitat, although it might be best to take a boat along the shore, as they wait on the Hudson Bay coast during the summer months for the water to freeze. Or if you stay around long enough, they might come and visit you! You could also take a boat trip to see the beluga whales. Unfortunately, the Northern Lights are only visible in winter, when it is dark. It stays light almost all night during the summer months, so bring a sleeping mask!

Anyway, I'd love to see you again. It seems ages since we last met. Stay as long as you like –

I don't get many visitors here! I'll even pay for your one-way ticket!

Love as always from your mad scientist son,

Darren

Hannah was thrilled at his reply. He had even offered to pay the price of a one-way ticket! Was he trying to tell her something?

* * * * *

The plane took off from Toronto to Winnipeg on time, and she soon felt as light as air, looking down on the Canadian landscape of green fields, pine forests and mountains.

Having arrived in Winnipeg, she changed planes, heading north to Thomson, where she transferred to a smaller plane for the final leg of the trip.

To the north, large expanses of snow reflected the summer light. The pale blue sky and white clouds were mirrored in Hudson Bay. Beneath her the snow was patchy with areas of green grass. As the plane lost height she could see a group of buildings dotted about at the end of a train track. Some were log cabins, some stone houses and others looked like caravans. Corrugated roofing covered the larger buildings.

As the plane approached the airport and the wheels touched the bumpy surface, her heart beat fast with excitement, knowing that Darren would be waiting for her. She wondered if he had changed much. He had moved to Canada 10 years ago, so he would now be 35 years old.

As soon as she stepped out of the door and stood on the top step, she experienced the chill of an Arctic climate, but after all, that is what she had come for, she told herself. When she reached the bottom of the steps, she stopped to pull out her sweater and put it on.

As she approached the Arrivals Lounge, she looked eagerly through the glass windows hoping to spot Darren, but they only gave back the reflection of a neatly dressed middle-aged woman with short, light brown hair, dragging her cabin bag across the uneven ground. There were very few people around inside the building. The whole place had a casual air. There was no passport control because it was a domestic flight, so she made her way towards the carousel to collect her luggage. And there he was, looking like a grizzly bear with his dark brown hair curling around his neck and his bushy beard and moustache. He was wearing one of those unironed red plaid woollen shirts that seem to be standard issue in Canada, baggy old jeans with no holes slashed into them and a pair of all-purpose brown suede lace-up shoes with thick crepe soles. He wasn't exactly fat, but had expanded sideways with increased muscles in his arms and shoulders. It must be the result of all that hauling wood and chopping up logs, she thought.

He held out his arms to her and embraced her in a bear hug.

'Mum! How are you? It's great to see you!' he exclaimed in a husky voice as he finally released her so that she could breathe. 'How was your journey?'

Holding his hand, she stepped back so that she could survey him.

'Really Darren, there was no need to dress up for the occasion!' she quipped in an effort to diffuse the tears of joy that were welling up in her eyes.

'You haven't changed a bit!' he laughed, pulling her back in for another hug.

He lifted her luggage off the carousel as if it were a Barbie Doll travel case and led her outside to his car. On the drive to his house, Darren gave her a guided tour of the settlement. It wasn't big enough for her to call it a town. He pointed out the entertainment complex and the general store where you could buy groceries and guns.

They drew up outside his house, which was just on the outskirts. It was a log cabin with a veranda. An enclosed porch was lined with heavy padded jackets that bulged from hooks on either side; she nearly stumbled over several pairs of waterproof boots arranged haphazardly on the floor. Darren led her into the lounge, where she was confronted by a shapeless dark red sofa with its back to the entrance. It had been situated to face a large stone fireplace, in which fresh logs were laid in preparation for chilly nights. To her horror, the wall surrounding the hearth was decorated with rifles, fishing tackle and the heads of dead animals.

'What's all that?' she gasped.

'What?' he replied.

'All those stuffed heads!'

'Oh, that was left by the last tenant. This used to be a hunting lodge. It was originally built by trappers who hunted seals for their fur.'

Darren managed to persuade his mother to sit down after promising to move the offending trophies to the basement.

'Would you like something to eat?' he asked. 'You must be famished. You know I'm not much of a cook, but I've managed to rustle up something for you.'

As they sat down to eat a stew of indeterminate ingredients, Hannah looked across at her son.

'Is there a barber in town?' she asked.

'Yes, only he doubles as the butcher.'

He stared at her light brown curls cropped close to emphasize the shape of her head.

'Why, did you want a haircut?'

'I was thinking more of you.'

She picked up a wedge of bread, which she used to mop up the gravy.

'Perhaps it's time to get your beard trimmed. With your rosy cheeks you look like a younger version of Father Christmas!'

He reached across for the salt, which he sprinkled lavishly over his food.

'People don't worry too much about fashion here,' he explained. 'They are more interested in keeping warm!'

'But supposing you met a nice young woman. She wouldn't know how handsome you are behind all that hair.'

He smiled.

'I've told you before. There aren't many available women here in Churchill. Two-thirds of the population are Native Americans. I work with several Inuits – they are great people, but they never introduce me to their women. I think the girls marry young.'

'What about European women?' she asked, swallowing down a lump of what might have been reindeer meat.

'It's a hostile climate,' he replied. 'Very few of them would be able to survive the winters here.'

'Don't you get lonely?' she asked.

'Sometimes, but I've got my colleagues at the research centre and I love my job,' he explained, chewing on a mouthful of food.

'The pay's good,' he added.

'Money isn't everything,' she countered, taking a sip of wine and putting down the glass. 'Why don't you move to somewhere closer to home?'

'Mum, I specialize in climate change. I have to work in the polar region.'

'What about Scandinavia?' she suggested. 'Some of that's within the Arctic Circle. Wouldn't you like a nice Swedish girlfriend?'

Darren smiled as he reached out for some more bread to dip into his stew. Hannah thought that he blushed, but it was hard to tell as most of his face was hidden by whiskers.

'Why are you so worried about me getting married,' he retorted. 'I thought you had enough grandchildren with Billy and Mickey?'

'Bobby and Mickey,' she corrected him. 'You haven't even seen them! They are adorable, of course, but sometimes they can be a bit boisterous.'

She looked away dreamily before adding: 'I wouldn't mind having a couple of granddaughters. They would be easier to manage.'

'I'll see what I can do!'

After dinner Darren lit a fire as the temperature was beginning to drop. He offered his mother a glass of sherry, and within ten minutes she was fast asleep.

Darren pulled a tartan blanket over her and kissed her on the forehead.

The next morning, she woke up to the smell of French toast sizzling in the frying pan. At first she was confused. Then she looked around and saw Darren in the kitchen, waving a spatula about.

'Hello, Mum. Did you sleep well?'

'Like a log. Do you have to go to work today?'

'No, It's Sunday, so I can show you the town.'

She sat up and was confronted by a dozen pairs of protruding black eyes staring down at her reproachfully.

'I'd love to,' she remarked, 'as soon as our furry friends have been removed to the cellar!'

The next task was to tackle her son's hair. She handed him an old pair of scissors she had found in the kitchen drawer. At first, he whined about having his beard trimmed until his mother confronted him with her ultimate threat:

'There will be no treacle pudding or Spotted Dick until you do!'

'Don't cut it too short,' he protested. 'I'll need it in the winter to keep me warm!'

'It's just short enough to frame your chiselled features!' she replied.

When she had finished, he looked at his reflexion in the mirror. He kept stroking his beard and surveying himself from various angles. He had to admit that he looked much younger.

His toilette complete, they both went out to survey the village. The centre wasn't far from Darren's house, so they walked. They made an attractive couple, and everyone called out their greetings or came over to be introduced to Darren's mother.

'Oh, is this your sister?' one old man enquired.

Darren pointed out the general store.

'You won't meet many eligible bachelors there,' he commented, 'just old men shopping for fishing bait!'

Darren took her into the complex that housed a cinema, cafeteria and public library.

'Oh good!' remarked Hannah. I was wondering what to do about reading matter. I've brought my Kindle, but I prefer hard copy. Will I be able to join?'

'That's all right. You can borrow my library ticket!'

'What's on at the cinema?'

'I think it's *Silence of the Lambs*.'

'Oh!' she exclaimed, pulling a face.

She was impressed by the hospital, a health care centre and a nursery all under the same roof.

'If you're feeling energetic, you can go to the gym, swim in the pool, play ice hockey or basketball,' enthused her son. 'There's even a curling rink!'

Hannah was beginning to feel the effects of jet-lag. She wanted to go into the café, but her son advised her against it.

'Why can't I go in?' she asked.

By now she was ready for a cup of coffee.

'Well, I don't think you will like the wall decoration. It's a polar bear skin complete with head!'

'What!' she cried, 'Someone killed a polar bear? They're an endangered species! It's against the law!'

'It was probably shot in self-defence, or before the stricter laws came out. It's been there as long as I can remember. Don't forget that this is the polar bear capital of the world,' he continued. 'Sometimes they come into town during the summer looking for food when they are unable to hunt seals. Now the townsfolk can only use tranquilizer darts to shoot them.'

'Hmmmn ...' was Hanna's response. Given the proliferation of firearms, she wasn't sure she believed him.

'If you see a bear on the street, you will need to get into a parked car,' advised Darren. 'The residents leave their doors unlocked for that reason.'

By this time, Hannah was ready for a sit-down. As they headed for home, they passed a museum which housed a collection of Inuit carvings.

'So you've no excuse for boredom,' remarked Darren.

The next morning Darren got up early to go to work, but Hannah was up ahead of him, cooking him breakfast.

'What time will you be home this evening?' she asked, flipping the eggs.

'About 6 o'clock. It's a 14-mile drive from the Research Centre.'

Sitting down at the kitchen table, he picked up his fork and bounced it on the edge of his plate: 'Of course, it takes longer in the winter when there is snow on the ground, but then I usually stay overnight. They give me a room and provide me with meals.'

He paused, looking over at the dishes that his mother was now loading up with sausages and bacon.

'So, what are your plans for today?' he asked.

'Mmmm I'm not sure yet – I can't decide between ice hockey and curling … .'

As soon as the door closed behind her son, Hannah cleared away the breakfast things and opened the doors to Darren's wardrobe. She pulled out all his plaid shirts and threw them in the washing machine. Then she cleaned the house from top to bottom, which wasn't too difficult as it was all on one level. There was an attic above, which she avoided, and a basement below, which she left untouched out of respect for her departed friends.

After lunch she had a siesta and then walked down to the general store to pick up a few bits and pieces. The cupboards and fridge were already well-stocked, but there were one or two items she wanted to buy for the evening meal. When she got home she ironed his shirts while they were still damp. Then she started preparing his dinner.

Darren arrived to find his evening meal on the table.

'Well this is a treat!' he beamed. 'Usually I have to cook for myself!'

For the first few minutes he was too busy shovelling fettuccini into his mouth to speak. Then he paused and looked up at her.

'This is good. You can't beat home cooking!'

'So, how was work?' his mother enquired.

'It was good. The same as usual.'

'What do you do all day?'

'I peer at a computer screen and make notes.'

After a few more mouthfuls, he stopped chewing again.

'So, what did you do today?' he asked.

'Oh, nothing much. I walked down to the complex and bought a few things.'

'Did you meet Mr. Right?' he asked.

'I'm not looking!'

When he had finished, he put down his knife and fork, sat back and pushed the plate away, his rosy cheeks glowing.

'So, what's for pud?'

* * * * *

The following morning, Darren appeared for breakfast wearing a freshly laundered tartan shirt. He kept looking down at it and plucking at the sleeves and collar, puzzled but pleased.

'What did you do to my woollen shirts?' he asked.

'I ironed them,' replied Hannah.

'I'll be the only man in Churchill wearing an ironed plaid shirt!'

He didn't know whether to be grateful or embarrassed.

'You look a real dandy!' exclaimed his mother.

* * * * *

Over the next few days, mother and son settled into a comfortable routine.

One day, Hannah returned from grocery shopping to find that the porch door was open, swinging on its hinges. She was sure she had closed it when she left.

She pulled the door towards her slowly, with one finger. The hinges creaked. Inside the porch, the boots were knocked over and in disarray, as if someone had trodden all over them.

There was a pungent smell that reminded her of zoos. She pushed open the door to the lounge, which was also half-open. A huge white head with coal-black eyes appeared from over the back of the sofa. A polar bear was lounging on the couch! He raised a paw the size of an enormous base-ball glove and beckoned her towards him.

'Come on in!' he drawled. 'Don't be scared. Sit down and take a load off your feet!'

Hannah nearly collapsed against the door post. When she had had a moment to recover, she blurted out:

'You can talk! I didn't know polar bears could talk!'

'Of course we can talk. All animals can talk. The problem is that humans don't know how to listen!'

Hannah's knees were shaking so she decided to take the polar bear up on his suggestion. She made her way round to the armchair where she lowered herself into its welcoming embrace.

The bear picked up a can of beer from the coffee table and deftly pulled back the metal ring with one claw.

'Here – have a brew!' he said in his gruff voice, holding it out to her.

'No, thank you, I don't drink, I mean I don't drink beer.'

'Go on – it will do you good. You look a bit shaky.'

Her mouth was feeling dry so she took it from his paw. She noticed the remains of a six-pack on the coffee table with the plastic rings partially removed. Some of the cans were open and there was beer everywhere, both on the table and carpet.

He took a swig from his can and she followed suit.

'Cheers!' he called out and she croaked something in response.

'So, what's your name?' he asked.

'Hannah,' she replied. 'What's yours?'

'Bruno. I don't know why. It means brown. I'm not a brown bear. I'm white. Well, in fact I have black skin and transparent fur, but let's not get too technical.'

There was a pause before adding, 'My mother must've run out of names!'

He guffawed at his own little joke and nearly choked on his beer.

Hannah managed to find her voice.

'W w what are you doing here?' she asked, clutching the beer can that had been dented by the bear's fist.

''Well, I was feeling a wee bit peckish – I hadn't eaten for 10 days, so I thought I would drop in for a snack.'

Hannah turned her head slowly to look at the kitchen. The cupboards and fridge door were open and half-opened packets were scattered all over the table and floor.

'Did you … did you find enough to eat?' she enquired politely.

'Not really, but it will tide me over for now. Thank you for asking.'

There was a lull in the conversation, which Bruno eventually filled.

'So, where are you from?'

'England, she replied, 'but I live in Spain.'

She wasn't sure of Bruno's grasp of geography.

'So why did you migrate to Spain?' he asked.

'Well, the weather in England is cold and rainy. I prefer a warmer climate.'

'So you are also influenced by the weather?' commented the bear. 'We have a lot in common!'

'Yes, well, the problem is, the last couple of summers have been too hot because of global warming.'

'Oh, yes? Tell me about it!'

Bruno picked up a half-empty can of beer and took a swig.

'So I've come to Churchill to visit my son in order to escape from the heat.'

'Did you come by plane?' he asked.

'Yes, I did,' replied Hannah.

'So tell me something. What kind of a carbon paw-print did you leave?'

'Well I don't know ... I ...' she spluttered, sinking back into one corner of the armchair in an attempt to make herself as small as possible.

'Do you remember lockdown?' was his next question.

'Well, yes, of course ... ' She was stunned by the extent of this bear's knowledge.

'Lockdown was great, at least for us bears. Most people weren't able to drive or go to work and do you know what happened?'

Before she had a chance to reply he answered his own question.

'There was a decrease in pollution and greenhouse gas emissions!'

Hannah opened her mouth to comment but the bear was in full throttle.

'In fact I composed a poem about it. Would you like to hear it?' he asked, getting to his feet.

He towered about 8 feet over her.

First he cleared his throat and then he started stepping backwards and forwards on his hind legs, in time to the beat. The rocking motion increased as Bruno became carried away by the poem. Hannah felt anxious in case he might knock over the coffee table or break something, but he was surprisingly limber for a mammal of his size:

My name is Bruno and I live at the North Pole
Where the ozone layer is just one big hole.
And because of green-house gases, now, the
        temperature is rising
The air and sea are warming up – it isn't so
        surprising
And as a consequence, the icecaps start to melt
It's hard to catch a baby seal or even a small
        smelt
When the planes were all grounded then the
        hole was getting smaller.
But we need to stop emissions now to make
        the planet cooler!

He bowed when he had finished and flopped back on the sofa. Hannah was so impressed by his ability to compose and perform his own poetry that she forgot for a moment that she was applauding a polar bear, and clapped enthusiastically.

'Well, that's so clever! You know, you really are talented … !'

He shrugged in a self-deprecating fashion.

'Yes, well … of course, lockdown is over now and humans have started flying again, so we are back to square one.'

He sighed and took another gulp of beer.

'Well, Hannah, it's been a pleasure to meet you, but I must be on my way,' he announced, peering anxiously out of the window. 'If someone calls the PBAP I'll be in trouble.'

'What's the PBAP?' asked Hannah.

'The Polar Bear Alert Programme are humans who catch polar bears and put them in jail.'

'Put them in jail? How is that possible?'

'Do you remember that big hut on the outskirts with a roof, rounded like a centipede? It used to be an aircraft hangar. They call it a Polar Bear Holding Facility. I call it jail.'

'I was wondering what that was . . . '

'They dart us so that we go to sleep and haul us off to prison.'

'How long are bears kept there?'

'Well, it depends. Usually for 30 days, sometimes longer. Most of us are released in autumn, when Hudson Bay freezes over.

'The females with young cubs are usually taken away by helicopter and dropped off on Churchill Cape. It's the young males that they target. There's no judge, no jury. Repeat offenders like myself often get a longer sentence.'

After a pause he continued:

'Churchill was built on top of one of our ancient meeting grounds, so the residents are trespassing on our property, not the other way round!'

'What do you do while you are in jail?' enquired Hannah. 'Do you hibernate?'

'Well, I sleep some of the time, but we don't really hibernate until the winter, when we've had time to build up reserves of fat. But they don't feed us! We're starving when we go in – that's why we come here in the first place!'

Hannah drew herself up.

'Well, it sounds very cruel to me. I can't imagine it's legal.'

'And what about all this ecotourism? People pay $11,000 to stay in some fancy-schmanzy viewing lodge, where they can gawp at starving bears!'

Bruno was getting more and more agitated:

'And of course they fly 1,000 miles from Winnipeg to get here! Someone's getting rich at our expense. I wouldn't mind if they tossed us a seal now and again!'

He rose to go.

'Have you had enough to eat?' asked Hannah anxiously.

He gazed at her with his soulful black eyes.

'I'm always hungry,' he said shrugging his massive shoulders.

She went into the kitchen and looked into the fridge. There was very little left inside. Scattered bones from a roasted chicken lay across the floor.

'I was going to give that to Darren for his dinner,' she thought.

'Did you try the freezer?' she enquired.

'Well, it has a bear lock on it, and I couldn't figure out how to open it.'

With a few deft movements of her fingers, the lock sprung open. She looked inside.

'It's all frozen stuff I'm afraid,' she remarked. 'You'll have to wait a while for it to defrost.'

She took a plastic bag and loaded it with a brisket of beef, several fish that Darren had caught himself and a leg of mutton.

She turned around to where Bruno was patiently waiting by the door.

'Thanks a mil!' he growled. 'I won't forget you.'

'Be careful now. Mind you don't get caught!'

He opened his arms wide.

'Hug?' he asked.

'Hug!' she replied.

As he wrapped his muscular arms around her, she learnt the true meaning of a bear hug. She had to tap him lightly on the back as a signal for him to release her, as they do in wrestling.

She placed the handles of the bag in his jaws, and watched him as he ambled off, away from the centre of town.

Even after he was out of sight, she stood stock still for a few minutes, thinking over all that had occurred within the past hour. She felt emotionally exhausted, and yet exhilarated. In a daze, she looked around. The place was a mess! She'd better start tidying up, she thought as she gathered up the half-empty beer cans. But then, what was she going to tell Darren? That a talking bear had given her a lecture on the consequences of global warming? No, it was better to leave things as they were and let her son draw his own conclusions.

She poured herself a brandy and collapsed into the armchair. She didn't usually drink during the day, but she felt she needed it.

About half an hour later, she heard the sound of heavy footsteps on the veranda and the squeak of the porch door as it was opened cautiously.

'Oh my ... ! Polars!' she heard him exclaim, and then, 'Mum! Mum! Are you all right?'

'I'm in here!' she called out weakly. He crashed through the front door. When he saw her sitting in the armchair he gave a cry of relief.

'Oh, you're all right! Thank goodness! Are you all right?'

He looked around the living room and into the kitchen through the open door.

'What happened?'

'I came home from buying groceries and there was a polar bear inside!' she replied feebly. 'I hid in the tool shed until after he had gone.'

He went into the kitchen and opened the fridge door. Hannah followed him meekly.

'He took the chicken. We were going to have it for dinner tonight!' she explained.

'Well, don't worry. The important thing is that you are all right.'

Then he turned to the freezer, which was shut but not locked. He looked inside.

'He took the brisket of beef, which was Sunday's dinner,' Hannah explained.

'But how did he open the bear lock?'

'He looked very strong.'

'Yes, but it's too complicated for a bear to open!'

'I must have left the freezer unlocked by mistake. I'm sorry …'

Darren pulled out his phone.

'What are you doing?' asked Hannah.

'I'm going to call the PBAP!'

'No, please don't do that!' she begged. 'If they catch him they may put him in prison! He said …'

Darren lowered his mobile and stared into her face. She was too young to be suffering from senile dementia.

'You do know that polar bears can't talk, don't you?' he said slowly and clearly.

'I mean, the man on the radio said that there was a polar bear in town ...'

'Listen, you've had a great shock. Why don't you sit down while I make you a cup of tea?'

The Buffaloes are Gone

The buffaloes are gone, all the buffaloes are gone
They've vanished from the skyline just like the
    sinking sun

They used to roam the rolling plains like kings from
    west to east
Now the land is empty; there's no sign of man nor
    beast

Millions upon millions, their great footsteps shook
    the ground
Now they are no longer, they have gone without a
    sound

Silenced are the hooves that once did thunder on the
    plain
The rumble of their cloven feet we'll never hear
    again.

The winter is upon us, but what will keep us warm?
Our tepees were all made of hide, a shelter from the
    storm

Only the sad wind whispers through the snow-clad
    trees
Who will clothe and feed us when the rivers freeze?

We live on reservations so it's hard to stay alive.
If we may not hunt or fish, then how can we
    survive?

It's easy to destroy us, the way is plain to see
Just take away our culture, our land and liberty.

NB: the title comes from 'Buffalo Dusk,' a poem by Carl
Sandburg:

Buffalo Dusk

The buffaloes are gone.
And those who saw the buffaloes are gone.
Those who saw the buffaloes by thousands and
    how they pawed the prairie sod into dust with
    their hoofs, their great heads down pawing on
    in a great pageant of dusk,
Those who saw the buffaloes are gone.
And the buffaloes are gone.

Carl Sandburg

Spanish Fly

Please allow me to introduce myself. My name is Fernando Mosca de los Peces Muertos. I used to live in a small fishing village on the Costa del Sol with my mother and 57 brothers and sisters. Every morning, just before the sun rose above the mountains, we would swarm down to the beach. There would be a buzz of excitement as the men pulled their fishing boats ashore and the cats would appear from nowhere and flow down from the cliffs. They would form a semi-circle around the boats as the fishermen unloaded their catch. The men would usually throw several of the smaller fish to the waiting cats. Once the animals had finished, we would move in and eat the leftovers. There was more than enough for all. It was a happy life, free of worries.

Then one day, I disobeyed my mother.

She always told me to stay away from the bus station. She said it was a dangerous place, and that on no account was I to fly onto a bus. Apparently that is what happened to my Uncle Alfonso and he never came back. But I was young and foolish. Now and again I would go there and watch from a distance as the red, white and green monster bus arrived. It was so big it could consume as many as 50 humans in one go. People would be spewed out of its mouth, and then more people would be sucked in. Then the doors would close and the bus would move off with a roar, puffing out black noxious smoke from its backside. It stank of diesel and rolled along on round legs, which meant it could go very fast. I used to wonder where the bus went and what happened to the people. The funny thing was, the humans used to wait around to be devoured by the bus.

One day my curiosity got the better of me. I landed on the shoulder of a man who smelt of an interesting mix of garlic and aftershave, and when he got onto the bus, I stayed put. Then the doors shut behind me and I was trapped! The bus began to roar and shake, and everything started moving, slowly at first and then faster and faster! I flew around in a panic, but the sight of the mountains, trees and houses whizzing by made me dizzy, so I tried to land on various passengers but they all swatted me. One man took a swipe at me with his newspaper, and a fat woman smelling of *Maja* soap wafted me away with her fan. In the end I returned to Garlic Man, who didn't seem to notice me, and I stayed with him until the bus came to a halt in Malaga. The doors opened.

When the man stood up and got off the bus. I followed him, but my delight at being free again soon turned to dismay and fear. I was completely disoriented. I had no idea where I was or how I would get back to my family. Worse still, I was hit with a wall of traffic noise, and the smell of pollution was overwhelming. Cars raced along and the people milled about. Everybody seemed to be in a hurry. The buildings were enormous, in some places blocking out the view of the mountains. Not knowing what else to do, I landed on Garlic Man's shoulder and stayed there, praying that I would somehow be led back to the peace of my home town.

The man went into a hotel and up to a room. We travelled on a lift, which was very strange. You went inside a big box with no windows and the door closed. There were some rumblings and shakings, not unlike the bus, and then the door opened and you were in a different place! By then I was completely confused. The room was quieter and cooler. You could still hear the traffic but the sound was deadened. Stunned by my experience, I drank some water from the wash basin and rested for a few minutes on the rim, trying to gather my thoughts together. I missed my mother so much I wanted to cry. I deeply regretted not listening to her advice.

After a while it began to get dark outside, although it remained light indoors. The man got ready to go out. I was nervous about going outside again, but I didn't want to spend the evening buzzing against the window, so I followed him through the door.

I sat on his shoulder as he walked through the streets, sometimes pushing past people who jostled him. The people of my *pueblo* have better manners. It was cooler now that the sun had gone down, and there was not so much traffic in the narrow passageways. Tempting smells came from the several restaurants we passed, but I was too scared to leave Garlic Man. Somehow I felt safe with him.

He went inside a disco and sat down at a table. It was dark inside with flashing lights, and the place smelt of smoke and beer. I felt a choking sensation, and the noise boomed out of the loud speakers. I thought I would go deaf, but after a while I got used to it, and even began to enjoy it in a funny sort of way. I had heard flamenco music and salsa before, and had even turned a few heads with my fandango. When you've got six legs, it's easy to dazzle your audience with your fancy footwork. They also played American music, which had a totally different beat – it was much simpler, but heavy and driving. I picked up the rhythm with no difficulty, and was soon grooving to the music.

To my relief, some other flies joined me, and we started to have fun.

'So, where are you from, Fernando?' asked a fly called Javier. He had an unusually high-pitched voice.

'I'm from Nerja,' I shouted above the din.

'Where?'

'Nerja!'

He turned towards his friends who all shrugged and shook their heads. 'Never heard of it!' he squeaked.

'It's a small fishing village just along the coast,' I explained.

'Fishing village!' screamed Javier. 'So that explains the smell!'

The other flies laughed, and I began to feel uncomfortable.

'So, are you guys from around here?' I asked.

'We are Malagueños!' he proclaimed proudly, and started to strut about and spin round so fast it made my head reel. The other flies cheered him on.

'On the subject of food,' interjected Francisco, in a huskier voice, 'I had the most divine *Boeuf Bourguignon* at Ricardo's today!'

I didn't know what *Boeuf Bourguignon* was, so I kept quiet.

'My dear!' shrieked Pepe. 'Have you tasted his *filet mignon* in a red wine sauce? It's to die for!'

I was a bit confused by this time, so I just concentrated on my dance steps. A live band began to play, and it was too noisy for any more conversation.

After a while, what with the dancing and heat and smoke, I developed a raging thirst. I flew around, but couldn't find any clean water. A man was drinking something that looked like muddy water with scum on the top. I took a sip from his glass but it tasted bitter, and didn't really quench my thirst. I looked round to see what my new friends were drinking.

'Here, Fernando, try some of this!' called Javier, who was drinking from a glass containing clear liquid with ice and a slice of lemon in it. I tasted it, expecting water, and spat it out in disgust. It had a strange dry taste, which only increased my thirst.

Francisco was savouring something out of a conical glass with a cherry in it.

'Try this, Fernando,' he breathed in gravelly tones. 'You'll like this!'

The cherry drink was sweet – much more to my taste – and I guzzled down several mouthfuls.

That was the last thing I remember.

I woke up on my back, several hours later. The place was deserted, except for a waiter who was sweeping the floor. The music had stopped, but my head was still throbbing. My mouth was dry and tasted stale. I felt awful. I thought I was going to die. Now the waiter was wiping the tables, and, as I didn't want to get swept off with a damp cloth, I struggled to my feet. Feeling groggy and confused, I made my way to the exit.

Outside I was dazzled by the bright sunlight, and the same hustle and bustle accosted me as before. It was hot, but I could smell salt on the breeze, so I headed off to the port, where I hoped the fresh air would clear my head. I got there and landed on a railing. After breathing a few lungs full of ozone, I began to feel better. Then I noticed a bus similar in colour to the one I had come on, but pointing in the other direction, so I flew onto it. I was greeted by the familiar smell of garlic, human body odour and Maja soap! This time I sat on the hand rail, patiently waiting for the bus to arrive in my home town. After a while I could recognize the familiar outline of the mountains. When the bus stopped, the doors opened and I flew out. I was overjoyed to be home again. I soon found my mother. She laughed and cried and scolded me, but I didn't mind. I was just glad to be home, safe and sound. All my brothers and sisters buzzed around in excitement to welcome me back.

Now I am old and grey, and my mother is long gone, may God rest her soul, but, young *chicos*, you should always listen to what your mother tells you. I've written down a little song that I heard at the disco. I can't remember all the words exactly, but it goes something like this:

> There is a house in Malaga
> They call it *The Bosanova*
> It's been the ruin of many a poor fly
> From here to Zaragoza.

> So listen *mis amigos*
> Don't end up with a hangova
> Or spend your life in sin and misery
> At the house of *The Bosanova*.

First published in *Al Gore goes to Heaven*

The Matador

My name is José Martinez. I am a famous matador. You may have heard of me.

A curious incident occurred many years ago that changed my life. I had been invited to perform in a bull-fight in Ronda, one of the most prestigious rings in the Province of Malaga. Upon arrival at a friend's *hacienda*, we had lunch. Shortly afterwards, my *mozo de espada* or sword-bearer arrived. Each of the three matadors are provided with a team of six men, the most important and least known of which is the *mozo*. It is his job to arrange accommodation and transport, take care of the matador's articles of clothing and provide him with various necessary items, such as the gold cape lined with vermillion silk, the smaller red square material used for close-work with the bull, and most importantly, the sword with which the matador deals the death blow to the animal's heart. A close relationship must exist between the matador and the *mozo*. The latter must anticipate his maestro's every need. The young man usually waits in the shadows of the alleyway, out of view from the public, but one glance or nod from the matador will prompt him to step forward with the required article. The matador is sometimes called the *diesto*, which means 'the right hand,' but I always think of my *mozo* as my right-hand man! I had not met Tomas before, because this was my first visit to Ronda, but he seemed like a trustworthy person, and we soon established the necessary bond.

He had organized a horse-drawn carriage to take me and the three *banderillos* to the bull-ring. The two *picadores* came on their own horses, of course.

We drove through the cobbled streets on a hot cloudless afternoon. Many of the inhabitants must have been still sleeping the *siesta*. Tomas took me to the dressing room, where he laid out my clothes. He handed me each piece of clothing one at a time. The last item was of course, my *traje de luces* or 'suit of light.' I looked at myself in the mirror as I adjusted my hat. The sequins on the scarlet jacket reflected the sun's rays that were streaming mercilessly through the window. The whole outfit was embroidered with gold, which only a matador was allowed to wear. The black skin-tight trousers emphasized my muscular legs and thighs. I was ready for my adoring fans!

I was glad of the shade of the tunnel as we passed into the arena. A brass band heralded our entrance. The *picadores* came first on their fine horses, both Andalusian pure-breds – one a chestnut stallion, who held his head high as his rider reined him in to accentuate the curve of his head and neck, the other a light brown with a blonde mane, typical of those of Arab blood. She minced around the ring, picking up her legs daintily as she went. I could hear the crowd cheer and applaud as each group of men emerged and paraded around the bullring. When I made my entrance, a shout went up as the spectators clapped and called out my name:

'José! Matador!'

The men waved and some of them tried to shake my hand as I progressed round the edge of the ring. And the beautiful women in their lace mantillas with raven-black glossy hair falling in curls to their shoulders threw down flowers and silk handkerchiefs before my feet! It was hard to choose. Then a green-eyed angel reached down and offered me a red camelia. I accepted it with a bow, tucking it under my bandana. A disappointed groan rang out from the other ladies around her, but ... what could I do?

Approaching the covered stand where the presiding dignitary sat with his wife, I removed my hat with a grand sweep and made a low bow.

As we assembled at one end of the arena, the horses flicking their tails nervously, my heart beating wildly in anticipation of the excitement and danger that was to come.

After a final trumpet blast, the crowd fell silent, and the first bull was released. He came rushing out of the enclosure, glad to be free of his confines, but then came to a halt, bewildered by what he saw in front of him. Our group of seven men stood on the opposite side of the ring, observing our opponent. He was a young bull, and seemed unsure as to what he should do. The two *picadors* pricked their mounts with their spurs, and the horses started off at a trot towards the bull. In those days the horses did not wear any protection as they do now, so it was as dangerous for them as it was for the bulls and toreadors. Sometimes the poor creatures would be disembowelled and had to be dragged off, along with the slaughtered bull.

Today they were lucky.

The first fight was soon over. The frightened young creature was easy prey. To be honest, I felt insulted that I had not been given more of a challenge to demonstrate my skills.

I withdrew from the ring while two other matadors took their turns. I was still shaking with excitement from the kill, and was glad of a rest in the shade of the tunnel, where I could watch my fellow bull-fighters perform.

When it was my turn again, I strode out once more to the tumultuous cheers of the crowd.

This time a full-grown bull emerged from the opposite entrance. He was a magnificent creature. They had saved the best till last. He was older than the first animal and larger. His muscles rippled under his glossy black coat, and he stood four-square on his powerful legs. He waved his head from side to side, snorting and scenting the air. When he noticed us observing him on the far side, he lowered his head and pawed the ground in a threatening gesture.

The two picadors set off towards him. As they approached, he walked towards them, preparing for a charge. Then, amidst a cloud of dust, he took off at a gallop. The two picadors separated to either side, in an effort to avoid his knife-sharp horns. Coming round behind him, they brought their horses within striking distance. The bull seemed confused by the unexpected attack from behind, and one of the picadors struck him between his shoulder blades with a lance.

While the picadors tormented and weakened him, I was able to observe the animal's behaviour. He favoured his left horn.

When they had inflicted sufficient damage to his neck and shoulder muscles, the *banderillos* moved in. Their job was even more dangerous, as they worked from the ground. Their task was to finish the work that the picadors had begun. By placing *banderillas* or pointed barbed sticks into the bull's neck, they attempted to destroy the muscles that enabled the bull to turn round quickly, making him easier prey.

When they had finished, I glanced over to Tomas, who was standing in the shade of the tunnel's entrance. He promptly stepped forward and handed me the gold cape. As I took it and shook it out in front of the bull, the folds flashed in the bright sunshine. The animal seemed bemused as I moved it before him. Again, he lowered his head and charged. I deftly whisked it out of his way, twisting my hips to the right. He lumbered forward and eventually managed to turn around. I twisted my body to the left, but this time he moved more closely, almost scraping me with his left horn. The crowd roared as I twisted and turned in a dance with the wild beast. When it was sufficiently angered and frustrated, I threw Tomas a glance. He took the cape from me, replacing it with a small red square or *muleta* and a wooden sword.

Now the Dance of Death began in earnest. Waving the flag before his eyes, I would twist my hips this way and that, sometimes stepping back to avoid the bull's needle-sharp horns as he charged at me. The beast became more and more enraged. The afternoon sun blazed down upon us, causing perspiration to trickle down my face, but I was intent upon one thing only, moving in for the kill. Tomas stepped up, sensing the moment, and placed a steel sword in my hands.

Weakened by the loss of blood that was now streaming down his shoulders and sides, and by the constant taunts, the bull hardly had the strength to stand up, but he would not lie down either. Leaning his side against the barricade, he left a crimson smear as he lurched forward. Now was my chance! As I advanced upon him, he looked up at me, knowing there was no escape. At that point, I could easily have plunged the sword between his shoulder blades into his heart, but something made me hesitate. Instead, I exchanged the sword for a dagger that Tomas proffered. Facing him full on, I plunged the blade into the bull's chest. He let out a bellow as his life-blood spurted over my jacket. I have killed many bulls and am familiar with that look of fear in their eyes as they realize that the game is up, but this one glared back at me in defiance with his blood-shot eyes. Slowly his legs collapsed and his massive body slid down the side of the barricade to the ground, but never for one moment did he take his eyes off me.

The crowd erupted in a frenzy of blood-lust. Many of the spectators waved their white handkerchiefs as a sign to the president that he should award me an ear. As I turned towards the presidential box, he raised one finger, which was the signal I had been waiting for. I bowed to him and turned back to my adversary, now a lifeless heap, with flies buzzing around hm. With one quick movement of my knife, I sliced off his ear, which I then presented to the green-eyed lady. As the mules dragged the bulk of the dead animal away, I paraded around the ring to the frenzied shouts and cheers of the spectators:

'¡Olé Olé!'

'¡Bravo, José!'

'¡Viva el matador!'

* * *

With the applause of the crowd still ringing in my ears, I returned to the peace of my friend's *hacienda*. After partaking of a hearty bowl of stew that my host's wife had prepared for us, I took my leave and retired early to bed.

As I removed my jacket and trousers, I recalled that they were stained with blood. Too tired to rinse them in water, I threw them over the back of a chair and collapsed onto the bed. My room was on the ground floor with double doors leading out onto a courtyard, where Miguel kept a fine stable of horses. I dropped into a deep sleep almost immediately.

In the middle of the night, I was awoken with a start by a clap of thunder. With a sudden gust of wind, the doors burst open with a bang, which was strange because I could have sworn that I had bolted them securely. The room was filled with a chill draught and the animal stench of the bull ring. In the blackness of the room, lit by sudden flashes of lightening, I could discern a bulky mass at the foot of my bed. As my eyes adjusted to the murky gloom, I thought I could make out a pair of blood-shot eyes glaring at me defiantly. With a shock of recognition, I realized that I was staring at the bull I had killed that afternoon!

The beast opened its mouth and a groan emitted from its slavering lips. It sounded like 'Matador.' This was ridiculous! Dumb creatures cannot speak! I must be having some kind of hallucination. It opened its mouth again and this time bellowed loud and clear, 'Matador!' I was reminded of the fact that the word meant 'murderer' or 'killer.' It opened its jaws wide so that its teeth gleamed in the half-light. 'Matador!' it wailed. I was afraid that its shrieks would wake up the house. And then it seemed to disintegrate before my eyes. With an icy gust, the doors banged close, leaving behind only the unmistakable animal odour. Despite the cool air, I was bathed in perspiration.

I don't know how long I lay there, clutching the blankets in terror, my heart thudding in my chest. I did not dare allow myself to fall back to sleep again, lest the ghastly apparition return to haunt me.

After what seemed like endless wakeful hours, a faint gleam of light appeared at my window. Slowly the black panes turned to a pale blue. I hastily rose and pulled on my everyday clothes.

I returned to my family farm in a village not far from Malaga, where we grew olives and avocadoes. I retired from bull-fighting, amidst protests from my lady fans and those who made money from arranging the events.

I never killed another bull.

PART TWO

The Collection

Old Tom and the Half Dead   107

Bobby   119

The Gold Coach   123

Meeting with a Stranger   127

The Torture Chamber   131

The House by the River   133

The Four Seasons   139

The Watchmaker   141

Casablanca   147

The Mystery Woman   161

Queenager   193

Old Tom and the Half-Dead

Autumn. Grey daylight fades into dusk. A gust of chill wind scatters the dead dry leaves.

Old Tom shivered as he pulled his shabby woollen coat tightly around him. Some of the buttons were missing and the cuffs were frayed. He should get himself a new one, he mused, but this one suited him for now. It had copious pockets. In one of them he had stuffed a bag of French fries that Jeremy at the fish and chip shop had given him. He could feel it through the worn material of his coat, hot and greasy with the promise of a full stomach. In the other was secreted a full bottle of whiskey which he had spotted in a van parked outside the pub earlier that day. The crate looked far too heavy for one man to carry, so he had relieved the publican of his burden by extracting one of the bottles and slipping it into the depths of his coat pocket.

He made his way up the hill to the church at the top. No-one would disturb him there. He could eat his supper in peace.

By the time he had reached the churchyard it was almost dark. A gibbous moon shone above the square tower, casting a faint shadow over the gravel path. As he opened the creaking lynch-gate, a barn owl swooped past him carrying something small and wriggling in her claws. He shambled past the graveyard towards the porch, his heart still racing from the encounter with the nocturnal predator. As he entered the porch, he was startled by a bat that flapped up in his face. He staggered back in surprise. He had to sit down on one of the two wooden benches that lined the entrance to the church, while he took a few minutes to recover from the double shock. It was a relief to escape from the blustery wind in the shelter of the porch. When he had regained his breath, he peered out. He could look down into the village where the lights were going on one by one as people settled down for their evening meal.

The church warden had obligingly left an oil lamp, which he lit, and pulling out his bottle, removed the screw top and lifted it to his lips. At that moment a gust of wind blew out the lamp and the owl, perched up in the eaves, let out an eerie hoot. He could hear the rumble of distant thunder. The starlings, who had already settled down for the night, flew up from the trees. Sensing that something was afoot, Old Tom rose to his feet and peered out over the graves, some new with marble headstones gleaming in the fading light, others coated with moss and lichen. As the clouds skittered across the moon, the tombstones flickered with a ghostly light. Almost imperceptibly, the top of one of the older gravestones appeared to move. Tom rubbed his eyes. He hadn't even had a drink yet. He must be imagining it. But as he watched, he saw, to his horror, a long bony hand pushing up the marble slab like a hatch. He stood, frozen to the spot, as a skeletal figure, all skin and bones, rose to a sitting position and, with his scraggy elbows poking out of the holes in his jacket, started to lever himself up out of the tomb. Once he had reached a standing position, he removed a battered top hat to reveal a skull-like head, smoothed down a few remaining wisps of hair and bowed.

'Good evening, friend,' the ghastly figure croaked. 'As you can see from my headstone, my name's James, but you may call me Jim!'

Tom let out a scream, threw up his hands in horror, turned around and scuttled back into the safety of the porch. In desperation he rattled the church door by its handle, but to no avail. It was locked. He swung round to face the spectre.

'W w what are you?' Tom stuttered. 'Are you a ghost?'

'Well, technically I'm dead, but I'm kind of stuck in limbo,' he explained. 'I'm on the waiting list for Heaven, but every time there's a place for me, something happens and there's not enough room.'

He let out a sigh.

'I died during World War I, but there was a traffic jam of souls trying to get into Heaven, and just as the Powers that Be were clearing out the backlog, there was a second world war, so here I am, still waiting to be called!'

Jim pulled the top of the gravestone down so that he could sit on it.

'So you see, I'm Half Dead, somewhere between the dead and the living. For example, although I don't need to eat or drink, I still have the desire to do so. In fact, it was the smell of those fried potatoes that awakened me from my slumber!'

Tom took the hint and tentatively stepped forward, holding out the bag of French fries. Jim took one, looked at it as you would a cigar and popped it into his mouth. He chewed it slowly, swallowed it, then helped himself to another. Tom thought he had better eat his share while there were still some left. When the bag was half empty, Jim wiped his mouth against the back of his sleeve.

'Mmmm, thank you! That was delicious!'

He paused, eyeing Tom's bottle.

'The only trouble is, it has given me a terrible thirst.'

'Here!' replied Tom, handing him the whiskey. 'Help yourself.'

After Jim had taken a few swigs, he wiped the mouth and handed it back to Tom with a sigh of satisfaction.

'So, how long have you been err dead?' Tom asked.

'Since 1917,' he replied.

Noticing Tom's astonishment, he added, 'Well, if you think that's a long time, you should meet Molly! She's been dead since 1848!'

'Molly?' Tom queried.

Jim pointed to a nearby grave that had a weather-worn moss-encrusted angel bending over it.

He picked up a stick that was lying on the ground and banged on the stone.

'Wake up, Molly, there's someone here to see you!'

As the gravestone began to rise, Jim grabbed hold of the edge and pulled it up. A wraithlike figure emerged from the tomb. Her wild eyes, surrounded by dark shadows, stared out from a deadly white face. Her long wavy hair, once a reddish brown, now brittle and grey, stood out in a shock around her head. Her arms emerged from a dun-coloured shawl, her long bony fingers spread out like claws.

Tom gasped at the apparition.

'Don't be afraid,' Jim said in an effort to calm the girl. 'Say hello to Tom!'

'My ticket!' she wailed, 'my ticket!'

'Show him your ticket, Molly,' Jim coaxed her.

She fumbled in one of the pockets of a voluminous brownish skirt and pulled out a small piece of paper, yellowed and crumbling with age, and held it before her, staring at it.

'We all get a ticket with a number on it, so that when there is a place free in Heaven, we get called,' Jim explained. 'She is very distressed because hers has crumbled and she can't remember her number.'

Then he added, turning his back on the distraught girl so that she couldn't hear him, 'To be honest, I think we have been forgotten.'

Tom addressed the waif politely, 'What did you die of, if you don't mind me asking?'

'I died of a broken heart!' she wailed.

Jim corrected her.

'You died of a fever! Don't you remember? You escaped from the potato famine in Ireland, but shortly after your arrival in England, you contracted a fever and died!'

Molly gazed around as if searching for some unseen object.

'If you ask this gentleman nicely, he might give you a murphy!'

Her eyes rested on the bag of chips Tom was still holding. He proffered her the French fries. She snatched up one and gobbled it down. Then she reached out for another.

When she had finished, she cried, 'I'm thirsty! I'm thirsty!'

Tom offered her the whiskey, which she gulped down.

Jim turned to Tom.

'She has a lovely voice! Give us a song, love!'

'What will I sing?' she asked.

'Sing about the green hills of Ireland and lost love!'

She started out softly, but the volume gradually increased. It was a haunting song, filled with sorrow and longing, and her voice was sweet and melodious.

By the end, Tom found himself wiping his eyes on the back of his sleeve.

When she had finished, the graveyard was silent. It was as if nature itself had paused to listen to her mournful complaint.

'That was beautiful,' blurted out Tom.

'She can dance too! Give us a jig, Molly!'

She turned to Jim and shrugged helplessly.

'There is no music!' she wailed.

Jim went over to another grave and banged on the top.

'Angus!' he called, 'come and play your fiddle! We have a guest!'

The lid of the grave opened and a tall gangly man rose up, dressed in a tartan kilt, a tam o'shanter on his head, a violin in one hand and a bow in the other.

'Come on and meet our visitor, Angus. Let me introduce you to Tom.'

Angus bowed and Tom offered him a drink, which he accepted. When his thirst had been quenched, he started to accompany Molly as she danced on the gravestone, her little clogs tapping away, turning her foot this way and that, heel, toe, heel toe, hands on hips. Then she grasped her skirts and whirled around. The wind blew, shaking the dead foliage off the trees. As the leaves whirled, so Molly turned and twisted and bobbed. Then she raised her hands above her head as her legs shot hither and thither in time to the music. When she finished, she was out of breath, but her cheeks were tinged with pink in what must once have been a pretty face.

'Well done!' the men clapped and called.

'But that was more like a highland fling,' commented Jim.

'That's because Angus always plays Scottish music!' Molly lamented.

'Show us how you do a jig!'

She took another sip of whiskey, glared at Angus and started dancing again.

And so the night wore on as the Half Dead ate and drank, danced and sang.

Imperceptibly the stars moved round behind the woods, which were outlined on the horizon. They faded as the sky lightened. At the sound of a cock crowing the three figures froze like statues.

'It's dawn already!' cried Molly, and they scuttled back into their graves and pulled the stone covers over them.

Tom, feeling both exhilarated and exhausted by the night's revelries, shuffled over to the porch and lay down on one of the wooden benches.

Someone was shaking his shoulder. His head was aching and he couldn't remember where he was. He blinked his eyes open, only to be dazzled by the light. The silhouette of the church warden loomed above him.

'Wake up! You can't sleep here! This isn't a doss house!'

The warden's voice grated on his ears.

Old Tom pulled himself up and shuffled off down the gravel path towards the lynch gate. As he passed Jim's grave, he paused and read the inscription:

'James Edward Sykes
1885–1917

Soldier

He died for his country
But he put up a good fight

He served his country well
And it served him right.'

He stopped by Molly's tomb, and deciphered what
he was unable to read by moonlight:

'Mary O'Shaunassey
1836–1853

Sweet little Molly
Her face like a queen
The niftiest dancer
You ever have seen.

A voice like an angel
She made the stars weep
Now she's gone from us
Forever to sleep.'

Angus' elegy read:

'Angus Malcolm Stewart
1875–1920

He was a great fiddler '

A thought struck Old Tom. He wasn't a religious
man, but he wanted to do something for them. He

turned around and walked back towards the church. The custodian was still standing in the porch, watching his hoped-for departure. As Tom approached, he barred the door.

'You can't come in here dressed like that!' croaked the caretaker. 'The church is for decent folks!'

'I want to light a candle!'

'You'll have to pay for it!'

Old Tom drew himself up.

'I've got money,' he replied pulling a handful of coins out of his pocket.

'All right,' grumbled the doorkeeper, stepping aside, 'but be quick!'

Tom entered the church. The morning sun, shining through the stained glass, threw dappled patterns of light upon the grey stone slabs. They shimmered crimson, gold, and sapphire.

He stopped before the bobbing flames, pulled out a few coins and listened to the chink as they dropped into the box. Then he took three new candles and lit them with a taper from an existing flame. He wanted to say a prayer, but he didn't know how. He looked up at a window above the altar that depicted a beautiful angel dressed in white with reddish-gold hair curling down her back and long, flowing wings. It brought him in mind of something he had read on one of the tombstones. Clasping his grubby hands together, he whispered, 'May flights of angels wing thee to thy rest!'

The church warden was still standing by the door as he left. Tom nodded to him in passing, then ambled down the path and out of the gate. A lark flew up from the trees, trilling its way across the pale morning skies.

As he hobbled down the hill, he reached into his pocket for the bottle. It was empty. He had a raging thirst. Rummaging in the other pocket, he brought out a few coppers.

'I wonder if the Fat Cat Café is open,' he mused. 'Perhaps Jo will let me have a cup of coffee!'

Bobby

The crowd roared as he raised the silver trophy above his head. His team mates picked him up and carried him shoulder-high around the stadium. There was whistling and cheering, and in one section of the bleachers, people started singing 'Rule Britannia!' Some spectators waved Union Jacks, while others brandished claret and blue scarves. The noise rose to a crescendo, and then faded and blurred into the buzz of an alarm clock.

Bobby opened his eyes. It was still dark. Outside the window he could hear the rain tinkling in the drainpipes.

He often had that dream.

He flung his arm out to the other side of the bed. It was empty. Then he remembered that Stephi was away on a flight.

Turning on the bedside lamp, he looked at the clock. It was 6.30. He would have to get up in a minute as he had a big job to go to on the Fulham Road.

After a quick shower, he wrapped a towel around his midriff, lathered his prickly chin with shaving cream and picked up a razor. Stooping his head to examine his face in the mirror, he noticed that the lines around his mouth and on his forehead were etched more deeply now, probably as a result of the time he had spent outdoors and in the sun. He still had his blond curls, although his hairline was starting to recede and there were a few white hairs at his temples, which were only noticeable if you looked closely. Tina used to say he looked like an angel with his baby blue eyes and golden locks. Ah yes, Tina. He often thought of her. He still felt guilty about deserting her.

In a way she was the perfect wife for a young footballer carving out a career for himself. She was attractive with her blonde hair, which she usually wore in a French pleat, not a hair out of place. She had good taste and style; she always dressed in the latest fashions and their house always looked like something out of 'Home Beautiful.' She was an excellent cook and a charming hostess. Although he had achieved his fame and success through his own determination and love of the game, she was definitely a driving force behind him.

Returning to the bedroom, he opened the wardrobe door and pulled out a neatly folded beige sweater from a shelf. Then he took a pair of sharply creased jeans from a hanger.

After getting dressed, he walked into the kitchen and put on the lamp above the stove. He didn't like strong lights first thing in the morning. The rain was battering against the window as he filled the filter with freshly ground coffee and poured in boiling water. When it was ready, he added some boiled milk and filled his cup, emptying the remainder into a thermos flask. He caught the toast as it shot out of the toaster and buttered it. Then he applied a layer of rough-cut marmalade.

As he sat down at the kitchen table to eat his breakfast, he fell to thinking about the divorce. He had met Stephi on a trip to Paris. She had hair the colour of dark chocolate that peeped out from under her red pillbox hat and framed her pixie face. He had invited her out to dinner, and one thing led to another. He knew it was wrong, but his career had taken a downward turn and he needed a soft place to fall.

He left Tina the 5-bedroomed house in Essex. The divorce was his fault, after all. His two children had already left home. They told him later that Tina had sold the house and had gone to California to start a new life.

He moved to the outskirts of London because he thought he would stand a better chance of finding work. Stephi carried on working as an air-hostess while he took a course in plumbing. He also thought he would be more anonymous in the suburbs. No-one expects the person who is mending their drains to be the Captain of the English Team!

His children rarely visited him now. Perhaps they still held him responsible for the divorce.

He looked at his gold Rolex watch. It was one of the few treasures he had salvaged from his glory days. It was time to leave. He always allowed an extra half an hour in case of heavy traffic.

Opening the fridge, he took out a package of roast beef and mustard sandwiches, which he had made the night before. He unwrapped the grease-proof paper and placed freshly washed lettuce leaves on top of the beef. He always added any salad stuff at the last minute to prevent everything going soggy. He put his lunch in a duffle bag, together with an apple and a bar of chocolate, slung it over his shoulder and went into the hall.

The street lamp outside the front door was still on. It shone through the stained glass of the demi-lune window over the door, casting pools of shimmering colours onto the tiled hallway floor. Bobby slipped on his leather jacket and picked up the tool box that was lying on the floor. He opened the door to a curtain of rain between himself and his grey van parked at the kerb outside. Pulling up the collar to his jacket, he stepped out into the downpour.

'Oh well, here goes!'

The Gold Coach

It was the 6th May, the day of the coronation. It was also the day that the cleaner came.

Charlotte asked her to start in the living room, so that she would be able to watch the procession later that morning in peace.

When the time came, she turned on the television. A golden coach appeared on the screen, drawn by eight Windsor grey horses, their highly polished flanks gleaming in the rain. It progressed along a street lined with flag-waving spectators, kept in place behind a railing. For some reason the scene had a muted feeling about it. Perhaps it was the grey sky. She peered into the carriage, but all she could see were two grey-haired people dressed in white. For a moment she was distracted by the cat, who had knocked her pen on the floor and was batting it around under the table legs. When she looked up, she could have sworn that she saw a beautiful young woman with dark hair and violet blue eyes, smiling radiantly and waving a white-gloved hand in an elegant gesture, her crown sparkling with rubies, emeralds and sapphires. Charlotte rubbed her eyes; she really needed to get new glasses! When she looked again, she thought she saw a lovely blonde woman, whose sparkling tiara was matched only by her dazzling smile. Then the figure seemed to fade. Of course, she had been mistaken. There was only an elderly couple, hardly visible through the rain-spattered window.

Charlotte called out to the cleaner, who was bent over the bathtub: 'Come in here, Maria. Do you want to see the gold coach?'

Maria left what she was doing and came into the living room, rubbing her hands on her jeans.

'Is it a centenary?' she asked.

'No, the king isn't that old!' Charlotte laughed. 'It's his coronation!'

Maria didn't seem very impressed. After a minute or two she went back to cleaning the bathroom sink. Perhaps it was because she was Spanish and didn't understand what was going on. Charlotte tried to draw her out:

'You have a king here, don't you? King Felipe?' she asked.

'Yes, but I'm not really interested in all that,' was her response. 'His father is corrupt and they spend a lot of money. I'm just a poor working woman,' she added. 'I don't need yachts and gold coaches!'

'Yes,' replied Charlotte, 'but the coach is old and it's being recycled. What are they going to do with it if they don't use it? Put it in a museum where no one will see it? Melt it down? Besides, it's not about gold coaches – it's about stability!'

Charlotte launched into her diatribe: 'Look what happened when you got rid of the monarchy here in 1933! It was replaced by a republic, which in some ways was good, because they threw off the shackles of a repressive Catholic church; women were given more rights and divorce was much easier. But then the anarchists started burning churches, killing priests and raping nuns! In the end they had to recall General Franco from Morocco to get the country under control. Unfortunately, it ended up in three years of civil war and 36 years of a brutal dictatorship, which lasted until Franco's death. Then the monarchy was restored, and Spain has more or less lived in peace ever since.'

Here endeth the history lesson.

Meanwhile, back at the Palace …

* * * * *

Charles and Camilla have returned to their private quarters at the Palace after the coronation.

'Well, thank goodness that's over!' exclaimed the new queen, kicking off her shoes and tossing her crown onto the bed.

She caught sight of herself in the gilt-framed mirror.

'Oh no!' she cried. 'My hair looks a mess!'

'Don't worry old thing,' Charles replied from his armchair. 'Your crown will squash it down. And don't forget, we still have to appear in public on the balcony!'

She flopped down onto the velvet couch.

'I'm dying for a cup of tea!'

With a sigh, Charles stood up, crossed the room and gave a tug on the bell pull, after which he switched on the CD player and started bopping around the bedroom, his crown skew-whiff on his head.

'And can you order some sandwiches while you are about it?' his wife shouted above the music.

All of a sudden, the plaintive wail of a woman's voice rose and filled the room; 'It should have been me!'

Camilla sat bolt upright and turned as white as her ermine stole. She looked as if she had seen a ghost.

'Turn that bloody thing off!' she yelled.

There was a discreet tap at the door. A servant came in wheeling a tea trolley.

Meeting with a Stranger

(The following story is set in the Elizabethan period. Queen Elizabeth, although a Protestant, was tolerant of Catholics. She had a mixture of Catholics and Protestants in her government.

However, she lived under constant threat. There were those who wanted to assassinate her in order to place the Catholic Mary Queen of Scots on the throne. It was the task of her spymaster, Francis Walshingham and her chief adviser, William Cecil, to uncover any such plots.)

* * * * *

As the door clanks shut and the jailer turns the key in the lock, I know that I have come to the end of the road. I look around at what may be my last resting place. A small slit too high up for me to see through sheds the only light into the cell. The stone walls are damp to the touch. At shoulder height I notice a crack between two of the stones that someone has chiselled out. It is not wide enough for me to see into the next cell. The sour smell of the previous inmate lingers in the confined space.

I shall not give in to despair. I drop to my knees on the chill flagstones and pray to Jesus to save me from what I dread most – torture. Under pressure, I might betray my friends. But I am here because of my belief in Him, and should be proud to suffer, and, if necessary, die for His sake, as He did for me.

The time passes slowly and the light dwindles. I hear footsteps and the sound of a chain scraping along the floor. The jailer unlocks the door to the neighbouring cell and speaks roughly to the new prisoner as he pushes him in and slams the door. Silence. Then I hear my neighbour's voice. He too is praying. I try to catch his words but they are muffled with tears. When the sobs die down, I place my mouth to the crack and call to him in a hoarse whisper.

'Friend, what is your name?'

There is a moment's hesitation.

'Daniel. What is yours?'

'My name is Gregory. You speak with the voice of a scholar. What brings you to this sad place?'

'My faith in Christ. I am a cleric who adheres to the true religion. For that I am punished.'

My heart soars with joy.

'Then you are my brother in Christ! I too am here because of my beliefs! I thank God that you are my neighbour, and that we can pray together and thus pass the dreary hours!'

'Who were your other brethren in Christ?' asked Daniel.

'Father Dominic. Do you know him?'

'Yes indeed. He is a fine man! Courageous and true. I have met him two or three times.'

'And do you know Andrew Fairfax – and Matthew Brite?'

'I have had the honour of breaking bread with them on several occasions.'

And so we talk into the night. The light is now dim, the tiny room lit by faint moonlight, but my heart burns within me at finding a like-minded friend with whom I can share memories of my beloved companions. Eventually, exhausted by the day's events, I fall into a deep sleep.

When I open my eyes again the cell is suffused with the grey light of day. I can hear the jailer's footsteps and the keys jangling as he opens the creaking door to the adjacent cell. He is a different guard. His tone sounds more friendly as he exchanges words with Daniel. Their footsteps echo down the hallway and eventually die away. I am left in silence, wondering why he has been released so quickly and where they have taken him.

Time passes. The jailer returns. I hope he will bring a crust of bread and some ale as no morsel of food has passed my lips since my arrest and I feel faint with hunger. My heart beats wildly as the warden unlocks the door. He bids me come out. My leg-irons clank as I follow him down the dark corridor, lit only by the flaming torch he is carrying.

'What happened to the other man by the name of Daniel?' I enquire.

'He's been released.'

'And what will become of me. Will they torture me?'

'I shouldn't think so. Not much anyway,' my escort replies, shaking his head. 'They already know all that they need to know!'

The Torture Chamber

Her captor led her along a narrow dimly-lit corridor until they stopped outside Number 13. Her heart was thumping and her throat dry. Was it too late to escape? She looked back along the hallway, where two men were standing by the exit. Just as she was about to make a run for it, the door creaked open and a bald-headed masked man stared down at her with his ice-blue eyes.

'Come in,' he remarked gruffly. It sounded more like an order than an invitation. She entered the room. By now she was trembling in every limb. What was he going to do to her? It was hard to see clearly in the gloom. The only light came from a long narrow horizontal window high up on the wall.

'Sit down,' the man barked. There was only one chair in the middle of the room, so, having given up all hope of escape, she sat on it. He opened another door and disappeared inside it. She could hear him washing his hands. Now was her chance! She searched around the room for a means of escape. Her eyes fell upon the skylight.

Although it was open, it would be impossible for her to climb up and squeeze through it. If she could attach her red silk scarf to it, someone might see it and come to her rescue …

The man came back into the room, wiping his hands on a towel.

As her eyes adjusted to the dim light, she noticed what looked like instruments of torture lined up on a table along a wall, glinting in the half-light. She was feeling sick to her stomach. Perspiration prickled her forehead and trickled down the side of her face. A sudden shriek pierced the silence. It seemed to be coming from the adjacent room. She clutched the arms of the chair in terror with her clammy hands. Before she could say anything, her torturer flipped a switch and a blinding light dazzled her.

He grasped one of the metallic instruments and came towards her, looming over her so closely that she could smell his musty body odour mingled with the sour smell of his breath.

'Here it comes,' she thought. 'The torture!'

'Open wide!' he muttered.

The House by the River

Poppy had been visiting an old friend in Bishop's Stortford, and on the way back, on the spur of the moment, decided to take a more picturesque route through country lanes, as it was such a lovely spring day. The winding path took her along lanes lined with blossoming hedgerows, past fields where sheep grazed in their cropped spring coats and their lambs sprang about the emerald grass. She passed through small villages she had never heard of with quaint thatched-roof cottages, pubs and tea shops. Along the grass verges daffodils nodded their golden heads and overhead trees shed their pink and white blossoms like confetti.

Soon she realized she was lost, but kept driving, in the hope that she would eventually emerge in a familiar location.

Then she spotted a signpost to Lower Gadding, which was for some reason strangely familiar. Then she remembered – it was where her family used to go on holiday when she and her brother were children, along with their three boy cousins and their parents. Her father and uncle would rent a house by the river, and that was where they would spend the summer months.

The memories came flooding back. During the daytime they would go swimming, rowing and exploring the islands that they came across on their expeditions.

In the evenings the grown-ups would sometimes walk to the village pub, leaving the children to their own devices in the house. They would play cards for ha'pennies or if it was chilly, sit around the hearth and frighten each other with ghost stories. Towards the end of the season they would gather blackberries and bring them back to the house, their arms scratched and their mouths purple. She still remembered the smell of the pies that her Aunt Mary would bake and the hot juice burning her mouth in her impatience to taste the dessert, still steaming from the oven.

With her heart in her mouth she followed the winding road that was almost dark with overhanging trees. The lane was so narrow that she had to draw up on the grass verge to let a tractor pass. Finally, she emerged into the sunshine. At the bottom of the hill lay the village where she had spent many happy days as a child. Of course, she hadn't been there for 50 years and much had changed. The car park behind the village pub was full, and there seemed to be signs everywhere. A modern supermarket dominated the high street. She wasn't sure if she could remember where the road that led down to the river turned off the main street, but she kept driving, and as if by instinct she found it.

Perhaps the house would be derelict by now, or someone might have knocked it down and built something more modern. The lane wound down and down, until she came round a bend, and there it was, standing intact, with a path leading through the garden and down to the river. It was smaller than she had remembered it, and more ramshackle, with paint peeling off the doors and shutters. The garden was overgrown with a tangle of briar roses and weeds sprouting between the flower beds. A lilac tree was in blossom.

Poppy could hear the river rushing by and a thrush singing from a laburnum tree. In the soft sunlight, it was like something out of a dream.

She wondered if the house was still occupied. Then she noticed that there were curtains billowing at the open windows.

Suddenly the back door burst open and three teenage boys rushed out and ran down the path, dressed in shorts and carrying satchels. There was her cousin George, leading the way! He was the eldest, tall and handsome with blond hair that flopped over his eyes.

'George!' she called, but he didn't hear her. He was the first to reach the river bank, where a rowing boat was moored. He grasped the tow rope and pulled the boat in line with the shore. Next followed Alan in his wake, with light brown curly hair. Then came her brother, Ian, with his white-blond wavy hair.

'Ian!' she shouted out. 'It's me, your sister!'

But he was intent on boarding the boat, and did not turn his head.

'I want to row!' he called out.

'You rowed yesterday!' Alan replied.

'You can both row,' interjected George. 'Just let me get the boat away from the bank and into midstream.'

He held the boat steady and Alan and Ian clambered in, but still it rocked.

A little girl with auburn hair emerged from the doorway. Her golden curls bobbed as she skipped along the path, followed by another small boy, whose silky blond hair shone like platinum silver.

'Wait for me!' he cried. It was Martin, the youngest.

George helped them both into the boat, and once they had all settled down, he picked up an oar and pushed the craft away from the shore. At first it drifted and got caught in an eddy, which whirled it around, but George managed to get it under control. There was much wobbling as the younger boys changed seats and took up their oars; soon the small skiff was travelling downstream, gliding along with the current.

Poppy stood rooted to the spot, listening to their shouts and laughter as they sped along until the sounds of their voices died away and were drowned by the roar of the water.

She stumbled back to the car, her heart heavy.

'Gone! All gone,' she exclaimed, as she slid into the driver's seat. By now her face was wet with tears.

'Martin was drowned at sea during World War II. Alan joined the RAF and was shot down over Îpres. George died of cancer, and Ian had passed away after struggling with leukaemia.'

'What was the point?' she asked herself. 'They are all gone.'

The sobs rose from deep within and shook her whole body, wave after wave. Gradually they subsided. She wiped the tears from her eyes, and, leaning forward, turned the key in the ignition.

The Four Seasons

Spring

Bluebells and daffodils beneath the fresh-leafed
    trees
Hawthorn in the hedgerows, the hum of bumble
    bees
A carpet of plum blossom, soft and thick pink
    flowers
Petals from the apple trees fall like April showers

Summer

The sweet smell of fresh-cut grass, lilacs in full
    bloom
Roses on the trellis exude their rich perfume
The rhythm of the lawn mower whirring to
    and fro
Coloured wings of butterflies, as bright as a
    rainbow
A winding path that leads me down to a cool
    dark pond
Where minnows, carp and goldfish move beneath
    the trailing fronds
of curling ferns and bulrushes; where dragonflies
    hover;
they dart and flit. Their gleaming wings reflect the
    golden rays

of dappled sun that casts its light through a
shimmering haze
A thrush sings out its trilling song, but soon the
summer's over

Autumn

The branches of the pear tree weighted down with
fruit
Wasps in apples on the ground, drunk with liquid
loot
A sharp nip in the frosty air, gold leaves slowly
turning
The crunch of dead leaves underfoot, the smell of
wood-fires burning

Winter

Now Autumn turns to Winter, a cold breeze blows
The fruit and flowers have vanished beneath the
ice-cold snows
The bare trees stand in contrast against the lowering
skies
Our Summer days are over. A chill wind moans and
sighs.

The Watchmaker

Chloë had often passed the mullioned windows of the clock shop on the High Street. It looked quaint in contrast to the other more modern buildings that flanked it. 'Clocks of the World' was written above the shop front in antiquated lettering. Today she decided to go inside.

She was expecting perhaps a gentle tinkle as she pushed open the door. Instead the chimes of Big Ben rang out; 'Ding dong ding dong!' As she closed the door behind her, the bell started to chime the hour: 'Doing! Doing! Doing!'

As she stood on the threshold, waiting for the vibrations to die down, she looked around the dimly-lit interior. To her right, the walls were covered with hundreds of clocks. Along the opposite wall stood a row of grandfather clocks of different sizes. Under a glass counter various watches were displayed, and on a shelf upon another wall were rows of alarm clocks.

'Doing!'

Between the chimes of Big Ben, she could hear the ticking of the other timepieces. They were all set at different times.

Then she noticed the clock-maker sitting at a small table in the corner of the room. He wore a round embroidered hat from under which his white fluffy hair sprang out from his head like puffs of cotton wool. With an eye glass in his eye, he was examining a stop watch that was lying in a dozen pieces on a white handkerchief.

'Good morning,' she ventured, fearing that she had disturbed him in his work.

Another 'Doing!' rang out, drowning her voice.

He looked up.

'Vill you be quiet,' he shouted over the noise, 'or I shall disconnect you!'

At first, Chloë thought he was addressing her. Then she realized he was talking to the door chime.

Only a gentle tick tock could be heard.

Then he looked at her, his face aged but his eyes bright and piercing.

'Good morning, Madam! What can I do for you?'

Doing!

'I've warned you!' he yelled, raising his fist in anger. 'I shan't tell you again!'

By this time Chloë was feeling somewhat unnerved.

'Yes, I'm looking for a present for my nephew,' she ventured.

He looked at her with sad eyes, shaking his head.

'I'd like to help a gracious lady like yourself, but I haven't got ze time!'

She stared at him, unable to comprehend what he was saying. The shop was empty, and in fact she had never seen anyone going in or out. She was beginning to understand why.

Suddenly his face wrinkled up and he started to chortle.

'Ha! Ha! Ha!' he laughed, his shoulders shaking. 'I am making ze joke!'

He opened out his arms, indicating the many time-pieces that surrounded him.

'I haven't got ze time!' he repeated. 'Do you get it?'

'Yes, yes,' she murmured, smiling weakly. 'I was thinking of a wrist watch, perhaps.'

He pulled out a handsome gold watch from under the counter.

'This is for someone who hasn't got much time,' he explained. 'It goes slowly!'

'No, I don't think so … '

Then he showed her a silver-plated version.

'And this is for someone who has time on his hands and is bored!' he chuckled. 'It goes fast!'

Chloë shook her head in bewilderment.

'No, no, that's not quite what I had in mind!' she replied, looking around the shop.

'What about a stop watch?' he asked, indicating the bits and pieces laid out on the table.

'No, I don't think so … '

'Do you know why it's called a stop watch?' he asked.

'No,' she replied, although she could have hazarded a guess.

'Because it has stopped!' he burst out laughing again, but, to Chloë's alarm, his hilarity soon turned into a fit of coughing and choking.

At that moment, something whizzed past her ear. She nearly jumped out of her skin.

'Cuckoo! Cuckoo! Cuckoo!'

She turned round to see a hand-carved and painted clock on the wall.

'Cuckoo! Cuckoo! Cuckoo!'

A bedraggled bird with bulging eyes and a yellow beak that opened and closed in time to its call shot out of a small door that had opened up.

She dodged out of the way.

'Oi vey!' cried out the shopkeeper, picking up a mallet. 'Enough already!'

By now, Chloë was feeling extremely nervous.

The old man hobbled towards the clock and waited, his weapon poised. The next time the unfortunate bird popped out, he smashed it with the hammer. The bird gave a final 'Cuck ..!' shivered and dangled limply from its metal attachment.

Chloë looked aghast at the shop keeper.

'Once he starts he von't stop!' he offered by way of explanation, raising his arms in a shrug.

By this time Chloë was at the front door, desperately trying to open it, but it appeared to be locked. All the clocks ticked louder and louder and started to strike the hour at once. A bell shrilled above the cacophony. The other sounds gradually died out.

She rolled over in bed and switched off the alarm.

'Oh no, it's time to get up!' she groaned.

Casablanca

This story is inspired by the film starring Humphrey Bogart and Ingrid Bergman. Here is a synopsis for those of you who do not own a television:

Casablanca is a love triangle, set against the backdrop of World War II. During that time, many people fled to Morocco, hoping to make an escape from Nazi-controlled Europe, either by air or sea. Casablanca came under German occupation but was administered by the French as part of the Vichy Government.

Rick and Ilsa meet in Paris where they have a brief flirtation. When the Germans march into the French capital, Rick flees south, hoping that Ilsa will join him, but she leaves him standing at the station.

A year or so later, Ilsa walks into Rick's *Café Americain*, a bar in Casablanca. As she explains to Rick, when she had met him in Paris, she had just received news that her husband, Laszlo, had died. He was a prominent member of the French Resistance, hunted by the Gestapo. She then found out that he was in fact still alive.

Laszlo accompanies her to the café.

Rick comes into possession of two exit visas, which were like gold dust to anyone trying to escape Nazi oppression in Europe. He offers one to Ilsa on the understanding that he would use the other one for himself. At the last moment, when they are all assembled at the airport waiting to board the plane to freedom, in a heroic gesture, Rick hands the other visa to Laszlo, and the couple escape with their lives.

Read on ...

* * * * *

Lisa gazed out of the taxi window at the flat landscape to her left. In fields of red soil and dry grass, skinny dark men carrying sticks guarded small flocks of sheep or goats; the Atlantic Ocean pounded the shore to her right. She could hardly believe that here she was, in Morocco, on her way to Casablanca, on her honeymoon!

She never thought she would marry again. Her first husband had been tall and dashing with film star good looks. He was charming and charismatic, and every time he entered a room the place lit up. When he asked her to marry him she thought that her dream had come true. But the dream turned into a nightmare. She was soon to discover that a wedding is one thing, a marriage another. Shortly after their honeymoon she began to see another side of his character. He had mood swings, going from cheerful and witty to irritable and depressed. His bad moods were exacerbated by drinking.

One day she asked him not to drink so much. He became furious, shouting at her and calling her names.

'Who do you think you are, telling me what to do?' he yelled.

He raised his hand, slapping her across the face. She staggered back, knocking over a chair as she fell. She picked herself up, and in a state of shock, retreated to the bedroom and closed the door behind her. She lay on the bed sobbing, wondering what she should do. After about 10 minutes there was a light tap on the door. Her husband came in looking mortified.

'I'm so sorry, Lisa. I don't know what came over me. Please forgive me.'

Unfortunately, it became a pattern of behaviour. He would always beg for forgiveness and promise not to do it again, but he always did.

She should have left him at the beginning, but she had no money of her own. After the birth of her daughter, she knew she was trapped. Two years later she had a second child, this time a boy. For years she suffered the beatings and the humiliation. Her daughter had married at an early age and had moved to San Francisco, probably in an attempt to flee from an unhappy home. Shortly afterwards her son left for college in Florida. Now Lisa was free.

One morning, while her husband was at work, she packed a suitcase and walked down the garden path to a waiting taxi, which took her to Newark train station. She got off in New York, where she melted into the crowds.

She met Richard three years later, at a New York film retrospective. He was not as handsome as her first husband – he was shorter and slightly plump, but he was kind and considerate and they became close friends. With his support and encouragement, she contacted her husband through a lawyer, and filed for a divorce. When Richard proposed to her, she was reluctant at first, but his easy-going nature, consistent patience and relentless compassion won her over.

Richard's marriage had not been a happy one either, but for different reasons. He had met his wife at high school, at the age of 12, and they had become inseparable. They married early, as soon as they had both graduated, and the first few years had gone well. His wife was a dancer, so they put off having children. But by the age of 30, she had contracted a muscle-wasting disease and was confined to a wheelchair. Richard spent the next 10 years nursing her, until finally she passed away. Although Richard tried to console himself with the thought that she was no longer suffering, his grief overwhelmed him. He thought he would never be happy again, until one day he met Lisa at a screening of *Casablanca*.

They had a small wedding in New York as Lisa had deliberately lost touch with the friends she and her former husband had in common. The couple had flown out to Malaga in Spain, where they had spent their first night in a hotel. From there they had taken a bus to Tarifa, where they had boarded a ferry to Tangier. The distance from Spain to Africa is only 8 miles, but it is across the Strait of Gibraltar, where the Mediterranean meets the Atlantic, and the waves are sometimes choppy. Exhausted by the journey and suffering from jet lag, Lisa began to feel seasick. They both stood outside on the deck where she was revived by the fresh salt air, but the blustery wind continued to toss the boat and blow her fine hair around. As Tarifa and its golden dome and lighthouse receded, Tangier came into view with its box-like houses and minarets. Soon they had disembarked, walking past the cars that were parked in the hold, which gave off the smell of petrol. Once through security and passport control, they emerged from the building, where their taxi driver met them and led them to his car.

They drove past tall modern buildings as the driver pointed out the French, English and Spanish sectors. In some ways it was not so different from a European city, except for the mosques and the signs in Arabic. Some of the women wore *jalabas* or long dresses with hoods or scarves covering their hair. Others were in modern dress. They soon left the traffic of the busy city and found themselves driving in the shade of palm trees past the walls of the King's summer palace and other grand buildings where the rich sheltered from the heat and pollution of the city.

It was late by the time they reached the countryside and were heading towards Casablanca; they watched the sun sink red below the Atlantic horizon.

Lisa had recovered from her nausea and was beginning to feel hungry. They stopped in a small town on the main street. There was no doubt now that they were in Morocco. The houses were run down and narrow alleyways led off from the main road on either side. Very few women were about. Men slinked around in the shadows or sat in dimly lit bars drinking tea and playing dominoes. They stopped and looked up unsmiling at the foreign couple as they made their way towards a restaurant. Inside the walls were decorated half way up with colourful tiles, but it had a run-down dirty look. The waiter insisted that they order from the menu of the day, which consisted of a vegetable soup, chicken couscous and a kind of flan. When they tried to order wine, the waiter frowned.

'No wine, only mint tea!'

The meal was disappointing but it was filling, and they got back into the taxi with renewed spirits. Their journey took them past swathes of countryside and small villages with only one or two lights. A crescent moon hung low in the sky, surrounded by a sprinkling of stars. After a while they passed a sign on the motorway.

'Two hundred and nineteen kilometres to Casablanca!' remarked Richard.

'How far is that in miles?' asked Lisa.

'Too many!' her new husband replied, squeezing her hand.

Half an hour later they passed another sign that read, '238 kilometres.'

'That's strange,' remarked Richard. 'We are further away than we were before!'

'There must be some mistake in the sign,' suggested Lisa.

Twenty minutes later another sign read, '257 kilometres.'

'We must be going in the wrong direction!' exclaimed Lisa. 'We just keep getting further and further away from Casablanca!'

'How can we be going in the wrong direction?' asked Richard. 'We are travelling south from Tangier along the coast road. The sea is to our right!'

'Perhaps we passed it without realizing and are travelling further and further away from it!'

'How could we pass it without knowing?' replied Richard. 'It says in the guide book that Casablanca is a busy port and the economic driver of Morocco! It must be a big city with skyscrapers.'

'Don't worry!' remarked the driver, holding up a finger. 'In one hour we shall be there!'

But in one hour they were no nearer. By now they were both exhausted and anxious.

'What time is it?' asked Lisa, waking from a doze.

'It's one thirty!' replied her husband. 'We should have been there hours ago.'

Now they sat in silence, huddled in the back, looking out of the window for signs of civilisation. After what seemed like an interminable drive, they spotted the glow of lights from tall buildings in the distance. Within half an hour, they were in the city centre. The driver turned down a back street and pulled up outside a four-storey building with the words, 'Rick's Hotel' flickering in pink fluorescent bulbs.

'Is this it?' asked Lisa.

There was one small light in the reception area and one or two windows on the higher floors were also lit up.

The driver dumped their bags on the pavement, and, scowling and muttering at the paucity of his tip, jumped into the car and drove off.

Richard approached the front door but it was locked.

'We'd better ring the bell,' ventured Lisa.

After a few minutes a bony dark man in a rumpled white tunic came to the door, pulling his white skull cap onto his ruffled greying hair.

He stood glaring at them as they brought their luggage into the lobby.

'What you want? You woke me up. It's 3 o'clock in the morning!'

Richard apologized for the late hour.

'I'm sorry. We had some delays on the journey.'

Taking out his passport and another document, he placed them on the desk.

'The name's Nicholls. Mr. and Mrs. Nicholls,' he added proudly.

The hotel manager squinted at the computer.

'There's no reservation for a Nicholls here!' he announced.

Richard opened up the sheet of paper and showed it to him.

'But there must be. I made the booking over the Internet weeks ago!'

The manager shook his head. 'There must be some mistake. There's no booking and there are no free rooms!'

'Oh no! What are we going to do?' exclaimed Lisa.

'Can't you phone another hotel for us and find us a room?' Richard pleaded. 'My wife is very tired!'

'I'm sorry, all the hotels are full! There's a big convention in Casablanca and people are coming from all over the place.' He threw up his hands in exasperation. 'Besides, I can't wake up people in the middle of the night!'

He paused before launching into a diatribe:

'All you Americans are the same! You come over here looking for Rick's Place, but there is no Rick's Place in Casablanca! If you want to see Rick's Place you will have to go to Hollywood!'

Lisa's eyes filled with tears. She tried to control herself but her shoulders started shaking and she burst out crying. Richard put his arms around her and tried to comfort her.

'Don't worry Darling, we'll find something!'

The innkeeper must have been softened by her tears.

'Wait a minute! I'll call my friend,' he mumbled grudgingly. 'He may be able to help you.'

He picked up the phone and dialled a number. After listening to the dial tone for at least a minute, they heard a click and a voice at the other end. The hotelier spoke into the receiver in rapid French.

As he replaced the phone he looked across the desk at the distraught couple.

'My friend, Captain Renault, will be here in a moment.'

He then offered Lisa a glass of water and shuffled off to get it.

While he was gone, Richard embraced his wife.

'There, there, I said it would be all right.'

Just as the manager returned with the water, the door opened and Captain Renault appeared wearing a police uniform and a peaked cap. He greeted the hotel owner and turned to the guests.

'So this is the unfortunate couple!'

Seeing Lisa's tear-stained face, he produced a clean white handkerchief from his breast pocket, and with a flourish, presented it to her.

'Dry your eyes, *Madame*. We'll soon put you right!'

He led them out of the hotel carrying their suitcases while they murmured their thanks to the manager.

An open jeep stood at the side of the road. The captain opened the back door and the couple climbed in.

The policeman drove off at speed. Fortunately, there was very little traffic at that time of night and they soon reached the suburbs. He took a smaller road that led into the countryside and again they seemed to drive for hours across a dark plain.

'Where are we going?' asked Lisa.

'Don't worry! We shall soon be there.'

They eventually arrived at what looked like a deserted airport. There was only one plane, an old Lockheed 12, but it seemed to be in working order as a pilot was sitting in the cockpit revving up the engine. The gas lighting gave the airport a sepia appearance like an old photograph. As they drew nearer, they noticed a couple standing in front of the plane arguing.

'I don't believe it! It can't be,' gasped Lisa. 'It's Humphrey Bogart!'

'And the woman looks like Ingrid Bergman!' exclaimed Richard.

The jeep drew to a halt and Captain Renault jumped down, again opening the back door to assist Lisa in climbing out.

Lisa and Richard walked towards the two film stars, who seemed too busy pleading with each other to notice them.

Lisa stepped forward and addressed Ingrid: 'It's all right to go with him. You're not married to Lazlo! He's only celluloid!'

Ingrid and Humphrey stared at her blankly for a few seconds, and then their faces broke into smiles.

'She's right!' exclaimed Humphrey. 'We're free to leave together.'

Hand in hand they ran to the aircraft and Ingrid mounted the steps with Humphrey's assistance. Then, at Captain Renault's prompting, Richard and Lisa followed and settled into the seat behind them.

They all looked down at the policeman standing on the runway and waved.

'*Merci beaucoup! Au revoir!!*' they cried as the plane jolted into action.

As it cruised down the overgrown runway, another car screeched to a halt next to the jeep. A German officer jumped out and aimed his gun at the plane as it soared above the airfield, but the bullets glanced off the side of the aircraft, causing no real damage. They left Captain Renault shrugging his shoulders as he explained to the SS officer how he had tried to stop them, but that his efforts were to no avail. His voice was drowned by the roar of the engine.

As the plane gained height, the sun rose over the horizon, fringing the clouds with pink. Humphrey Bogart turned in his seat, his arm around Ingrid, and with a crooked grin called out, 'California, here we come!'

The Mystery Woman

London, 1944

I dreamt I was trapped in a deep well. There was a large stone at the bottom which I was trying to lift, but it was too heavy. I started to float up to the top, but the circle of sky above me was as grey as lead. I opened my eyes. The pale morning light filtered through a crack in the black-out curtains. I was home again.

There had been no air-raids during the night to interrupt my deep sleep, which had been brought on by a feeling of utter exhaustion.

Then I remembered. My hands slid down to my stomach. I had lost my baby. A stab of searing grief clutched at my heart. When I thought of the soft pink body in my arms smelling of warm milk, the tears started to roll down my cheeks. What was I going to tell Harold, away in France fighting the war? He too had longed for our first child. He had hoped for a girl, and that was what I had delivered, but after three days the infant began to sicken. She didn't want to take her milk and there was a bluish pallor about her eyes. The nurses placed her in an incubator, but after another two days the baby showed no signs of improvement and, on the sixth day, God saw fit to take her. I had been sent as an evacuee to Sheffield, but there was no point in me staying any longer, so as soon as I was pronounced strong enough by the doctors, I left the hospital and took the long train journey back to London.

How was I going to face the day? I didn't feel hungry, but I knew I needed to eat something. I dragged myself out of bed and made my way to the kitchenette. There wasn't much food left in the flat after my long absence. I found some oats at the back of the cupboard, which I boiled up into porridge, and made myself a cup of Camp coffee, using tinned milk.

I would have to go out shopping soon, but I didn't feel ready to face the world. The good thing about living in London was that you were anonymous. Nobody knew anybody. I wouldn't have to face a curious neighbour or a family member asking solicitously, 'So what happened to your baby?'

I pulled on an old cardigan over my jumper. My shoes were worn and shabby. I caught a glimpse of myself in the mirror as I walked towards the door. My fair hair hung limply around my thin face and my eyes were hollowed out with dark shadows around them.

Even though it was August, it felt more like a damp winter's day. There weren't many people on the streets as I made my way to the grocer's. Most of the men were away fighting the war. Those who were left, if they were lucky, had fled alone or with their families to the smaller towns or countryside where they were less likely to be the target of bombs. As I passed several bombsites where houses had once stood, I thought of all the people who had died. In spite of the deserted streets, there was a queue outside the grocery shop, women with scarves around their heads hugging empty shopping bags. I still had some coupons left because I hadn't used them while I was in hospital. I was able to buy some butter, bread, cheese, tinned milk, tea and dried egg powder. I couldn't help thinking of the freshly laid eggs that I had eaten for breakfast on the farm in Yorkshire where I had stayed.

On the way to the greengrocer's, a woman passed by me pushing a pram. I had to avert my eyes that were fast filling with tears. After waiting in line again, I left with some potatoes and half a cabbage.

On the way home a blood-curdling wail blasted my ears. The air-raid siren had gone off. I hadn't heard one for several months, which made it even more threatening. I felt sick with fear as I rushed to the nearest underground station. The stench of human bodies packed closely together turned my stomach as I descended the steps. The station was crowded with people either sitting or standing. Some had blankets and were surrounded by their few personal belongings. I crouched down against the wall, not wanting to get my clothes dirty by sitting on the ground. As I squatted, waiting for the first doodle bug to drop, I looked around me at the different figures in the dim light. The scene made me think once more of the village I had left behind, with its green hills and fields where animals grazed. Then I remembered the child I had lost, and started weeping uncontrollably.

'Cheer up, love!' chirped a voice to my left. 'Don't let the buggers get you down!'

I turned my head to see a middle-aged woman with straggly blonde hair holding out a packet of biscuits.

'Here, have a Rich Tea!'

I took one, mumbling my thanks, then leant back against the wall nibbling at it as the tears streamed down my cheeks.

'When will it end?' I thought, 'What is the point of it all?'

I was startled out of my gloomy thoughts by the distinctive whine of a doodle bug. In the eery silence that ensued, everybody started counting: 'Ten, nine, eight, seven, six ...' Shortly after they reached 'one,' I heard a dull thud. We all sat in silence, imagining the fire-bomb bursting into flames, wondering whose house had been hit.

When the 'all clear' finally sounded, everyone gave a sigh of relief. Most of the crowd made their way to the exit, although some stayed behind because they had no-where else to go.

It was dusk by the time I emerged from the underground station. Even though it was chilly, I was glad to breathe in the relatively fresh air after the stagnant atmosphere of the shelter. I looked around to survey the damage. Several plumes of smoke arose in the streets around me. As I made my way home, I caught sight of a building in flames at the end of the street. Firefighters were already hosing it down, and a small crowd of people had gathered on the pavement outside. I joined the homeless tenants and other passers-by to watch as part of the façade crumbled. Then I heard the sound of a baby crying above the roar of the fire and the hiss of water on flames. Without thinking, I put down my shopping bag and ran towards the front door. A warden barred my way.

'Sorry Miss, you can't go inside. It's much too dangerous!'

I backed away from his outstretched arms, and, looking around, spotted a space further down where part of the wall had collapsed. I entered the burning house before anyone could stop me. Once inside, I stood at the bottom of the staircase, where I could hear the baby's cries above me. By now, the flames were engulfing the middle area and the place was filling with smoke. I rushed up the stairs to the first floor. Screams were coming from a room halfway along the passage as flames licked around the door in a circle of fire. I looked around in desperation, the smoke now choking my lungs. At the end of the hallway at the back of the building I noticed a door that was standing ajar. I rushed up to it and pushed it open to reveal a bathroom. Grabbing a towel, I turned on the tap and, after dipping it in water and wringing it out, I wrapped it around my face. I dashed back to the flaming door, beyond which the baby was now shrieking hysterically. Without a second thought, I lifted my foot, and kicked in the middle part of the door. At first, I could not see anything as the room was full of smoke. Guided by the screams I moved towards an orange box, where a baby was lying wrapped in a knitted shawl. I snatched it up, and clutching the infant to me, made my way down the stairs. By now the front of the building was a wall of fire, and girders were crashing around me. The heat was unbearable. I rushed to the back, where I found a door that opened onto another bathroom. The window was half-open. Still holding on tight to the baby, I jerked it up with my free hand and climbed out into the back garden. I stood for a moment, gasping in the cool evening air. Looking around, I spotted a garden gate to my right. I opened it and found myself in an alleyway that ran along the side of the building. What should I do? Should I return to the chaos at the front of the house, or should I take a short-cut home? By now the child's screams had subsided. It must have sensed the security of my arms. Only a blubbering sound emitted from the bundle that I was carrying. As I hurried along the deserted back streets, the baby started crying again. It was probably hungry. I looked around. Someone might stop me. But who would notice a woman with a baby heading home before the curfew?

When I reached the safety of my one-bedroom flat, I closed the door behind me, switched on the light and leaned against the wall, still clutching the infant tightly. I was shaking all over, possibly from the shock of the bombing raid and from entering the blazing building, but I also felt exhilarated from the rescue of the baby. I sat down on the sofa and unwrapped the bundle on my lap. Underneath the purple and pink shawl lay a perfect little girl several weeks old with dimples in her knees and dark wispy hair. As she started to cry again, I lifted her to my breast and began nursing her. A sense of peace descended upon me. When the baby had finished, she fell asleep with a bubble of milk at the corner of her mouth. I sat there for a while, still holding her in my arms and gazing down at her. Finally, I lay her down in the cot, the one I had bought for my own child.

I got up and closed the black-out curtains. Then I put on the kettle to make myself some tea. It was only at that point that I realized that I had left my shopping outside the building! There was no point in going back for it. It would be gone by now! Never mind, I had returned with something far more precious! I made myself a cup of coffee instead and chewed on a couple of dry biscuits. The room was cold and damp, so I lit a fire with the few sticks of wood that I still had in reserve.

After lighting a couple of candles on the mantelpiece, I turned off the light and sat gazing at the sleeping child by firelight. She had the face of an angel. But what should I do with her? I should return her to her mother, but I didn't know who her mother was. She was no doubt a tenant of the building, but now the rooms were unfit for habitation. Judging by the makeshift cradle, the mother must have been poor, but then everyone was after five years of war. I came to the conclusion that the woman was probably unmarried. The father was most likely off fighting the war like my own husband. Perhaps the child was the product of a wartime romance during which a serviceman might persuade a woman to succumb to his charms before leaving for the Continent, not knowing if or when he would come back. It happened all the time. But it was irresponsible of the mother to go out and leave an infant unattended; still, what else was she to do if she was on her own? I looked around my cosy home and thought that I was probably luckier than most. In the end I persuaded myself that the baby would be better off with me. But what would I tell my husband? I looked up at his photograph on the mantelpiece. It occurred to me that he need never know that the baby wasn't his. The girl was only a week or so older than my own child would have been and I still had the birth certificate! The new baby could assume Cleo's identity! God had taken away my baby, but had given me another one in her place!

The next morning, after feeding the baby and changing her nappy, I went out to replenish the groceries that I had left outside the burning building, at least as far as my coupons and money would stretch. On the way back, I passed a newsagent's that had on a box outside the headlines of the local paper: 'Mystery Woman enters burning building to save baby!'

I bought a copy and stood on the pavement reading the report.

A 'Mystery Woman' braved the flames and rushed into a recently bombed block of flats at No. 29 Gresham Street because, she said, she could hear a baby crying. The warden tried to stop her but she entered by a hole in the wall. She disappeared into the burning building and no trace was found of either her or the alleged baby.

'The landlady said, "There couldn't have been a baby because no children are allowed. It must have been a cat meowing." '

January 1945

The baby's crying woke me up. I reached down to the cot beside my bed and picked Cleo up, who quietened down as soon as I started feeding her. She was an easy child. As the sun rose, spreading its rays across the carpeted floor, I smiled to myself.

'Today is a special day!' I announced, looking down at the infant. 'Daddy's coming home!'

The baby gurgled.

I got up and put on a pink blouse and navy-blue skirt, my 'best clothes' that I had been saving for a special occasion. I arranged my hair in waves and put on a touch of lipstick.

The rest of the morning I spent fidgeting around the flat, making sure that it was clean and tidy. I must have picked up Cleo a dozen times, telling her excitedly, 'Daddy's coming home!'

But I was also a little apprehensive. Would he be able to tell that Cleo was not his child? But that was absurd. How would he know?

I had managed to get hold of a tin of corned beef that I had mixed with fried onions and a tin of tomatoes. I planned to serve it with mashed potatoes. It would be filling, at least. I kept looking out of the window for a dark-haired man in army fatigues.

At around 2 o'clock, just as I was beginning to feel hungry and was wondering how long I should postpone lunch, there was a ring of the doorbell.

My heart racing, I rushed to the door, pausing briefly to check my hair in the wall mirror as I went. When I opened the door, there he stood, tall, dark and handsome. He was wearing his army uniform and was carrying a rucksack, which he put down on the floor just inside the flat. Then he removed his peaked cap, which he threw down on the sofa, and took me in his arms.

'Lillian, darling, it's so good to see you again!' he murmured, clutching me to him. 'I thought this moment would never come!'

'Harold! It's so wonderful to have you home at last!' I cried, tears of joy rolling down my cheeks. 'It's been so long!'

After the first embrace, Harold stepped back to take a look at me.

'You're as pretty as ever!' he exclaimed.

I noticed that his face was more lined, he was thinner and there was a weariness in his eyes.

'You're still the handsome man I married!' I assured him.

'And the baby?' he asked, looking around.

'Through here,' I replied, taking his hand and leading him to the bedroom. Cleo was sleeping soundly in her cot.

'She's so beautiful!' he exclaimed. He crouched down and gazed at her adoringly, his face full of wonder.

'She has your dark hair,' I remarked.

'And your rosy cheeks!' he replied.

'Go ahead! You can pick her up.'

Harold hesitated.

'But she's asleep!'

I leant over the side of the cot and hauled her up under the armpits, placing her in his arms.

The tiny child looked incongruous in the big man's arms, but she opened her eyes and looked at him. He stood looking down at her, his face shining with pride.

When he finally laid her back in her cot, he turned to me.

'What's for dinner? I'm famished!'

I dished up the lunch, which Harold tucked into with enthusiasm.

'It's the best I could do,' I remarked apologetically. 'You know what it's like with the shortages.'

'It's delicious,' replied Harold looking up from his plate with a grin. 'You should try army food!'.

For dessert, I had wanted to make him some kind of sponge pudding, but without fresh eggs, it was impossible to do, so instead, I opened a tin of peaches and poured evaporated milk over them.

Harold's face glowed.

'It's great to be home!' he said, reaching across the table and taking my hand.

<u>May 1959</u>

It was a lovely spring morning. Harold came over to me as I was clearing away the breakfast plates. He kissed me on the cheek.

''Bye love! I might be a bit late coming home this evening,' he explained, adjusting his bowler hat in the hall mirror.

'I've got a pile of work to do!'

Cleo came clumping down the stairs carrying her satchel over her shoulder.

'Hurry up, dear,' I called. 'You'll be late for school!'

''Bye Mum!' she shouted back as she dashed out of the front door, following her father down the garden path to the car.

I stood at the threshold of the front door and waved goodbye as the car pulled away from the kerb.

When I had finished the washing up, I made myself a cup of coffee and sat down at the dining room table. Looking out at the birds as they flitted from one tree to another, I thought how lucky I was. I lived in a lovely three-bedroom house in the suburbs of London – the so-called 'Green Belt,' – I had a wonderful husband and a beautiful daughter who was easy-going and did well at school – ah, Cleo! In all these 15 years, no-one had guessed my secret!

The phone rang at about 2 p.m. There was a man's voice that I did not recognize on the other end of the line.

'Mrs. Benson?'

'Yes, speaking.'

'I'm calling from your husband's office.'

He hesitated.

My heart gave a lurch.

'Yes?'

'I'm afraid I have some bad news.' He paused. 'Harold has been taken ill with severe stomach pains. He has been taken to the hospital in an ambulance.'

I was silent for a moment while I absorbed his words.

'Mrs. Benson?'

'Yes, I'm sorry. I'm just a bit shocked.'

I caught sight of my blanched face in the mirror.

'Which hospital was he taken to?'

'The Royal Infirmary'

'Thank you, yes, thank you. I'll go right away!'

I felt numb as I put the phone down. What was I to do? I didn't have a car. I could ring for a taxi or take a bus, but it must have been urgent, otherwise his colleague would not have called. I took a taxi.

The driver dodged through heavy traffic honking his horn at late-lunchers returning to work. When I reached the hospital, I was sent to the Emergency Unit. I was told by the nurse that I should wait outside until the doctor came to speak to me.

Why wouldn't they let me see him? Perhaps he was having an operation. But he was never ill. What could be wrong with him?

The door swung open and closed several times, but no member of staff came out to speak to me. I kept glancing at the wall clock, but the hands barely seemed to move.

After an agonizingly long wait, the doctor appeared, his white coat flapping. He sat down beside me and put his elbows on his knees, his hands clasped in front of him.

'I'm sorry, Mrs. Benson. I have some bad news for you.'

He looked down at his white knuckles before continuing.

'Your husband had to have an appendectomy, and during the operation, his appendix burst.'

I could hardly take in what he was saying.

'You mean, my husband is … ?'

'I'm very sorry. There was nothing we could do to save him.'

He directed me to an office where I could pick up his death certificate. While I was waiting, a nurse came along with his clothes in a bag. I was dry-eyed and numb, in a state of shock.

'Cleo will be home soon,' I thought. 'What shall I tell her?'

During the next few days, I stumbled from one place to another, like a drunken robot. Cleo took time off school and came with me. We went to the registrar and then to the funeral parlour. All the time I kept repeating to myself, 'Harold is dead!' but it didn't make any sense to me. Both Cleo and I were devastated by his sudden demise. Cleo had always adored her father.

The next few months passed in a blur. Seeing how much Cleo missed her father, I fell to thinking about the girl's natural parents. Perhaps it was time to tell her the truth, now that I no longer had to hide anything from my husband.

One morning, Cleo wandered into the dining room looking pale and red-eyed.

'Sit down, Cleo. I have something to tell you.'

When I had finished, Cleo looked at me blankly.

'I can't believe what you are saying! You mean that Daddy isn't my real father?'

'That's correct.'

'And you're not my real mother!'

Cleo stared at me, almost belligerently.

'We were your foster parents, but we brought you up as our own.'

I went to a drawer and brought out the yellowed newspaper report to show her. She had to read it several times before she could take in the information.

'So you are the Mystery Woman!' she exclaimed in disbelief.

'I saved your life!' I explained. 'I did everything out of love for you!'

'And my real mother? She doesn't know I exist!'

'It was during the war. Everything was in chaos.'

I gave a helpless shrug. 'It was hard to trace people.'

Cleo sat staring at the article in silence. Then she looked up.

'Then my real father might still be alive?'

'That's a possibility. But remember, Daddy loved you like his own daughter. He provided for you and protected you.'

I cleared up the dishes and took them into the kitchen. When I came back, Cleo had disappeared into her bedroom and had shut the door.

'Perhaps the shock was too much for her,' I thought.

I called her down for lunch, but she did not appear. I took a tray of soup and a sandwich up to her bedroom and placed it outside her door. I knocked softly. No answer.

'There's some food outside your door,' I called gently. 'Don't let the soup get cold!'

The next time I went upstairs, I noticed that the tray was still there with the food untouched.

Later in the afternoon, Cleo came downstairs looking truculent, as only a teenager can do.

'I'm just putting the kettle on. Would you like a cup?'

Cleo didn't answer, so I made tea for two and placed some biscuits on a plate.

When I brought in the tea things, Cleo was sitting on the couch, clutching a crumpled handkerchief on her lap. As I placed the tray on the coffee table, Cleo suddenly burst into tears. I went to sit down beside her. Cleo threw her arms round my neck.

'I'm so sorry, Mummy!' she sobbed. 'I'm so confused! I miss Daddy so much, and now this news about my birth parents!'

'I know, darling. It's a lot to take in, but I thought you should know.'

I sat stroking her hair.

'I want to find my real father,' she blurted out.

'Well, I can understand that!'

After a pause, during which Cleo blew her nose, I continued: 'Listen, I can't let you walk around the streets of London by yourself, ringing other people's doorbells. I'll come with you. We'll find him together. All right?'

'All right,' she replied, sniffing and wiping her eyes.

I gave her a hug. Before Cleo could change her mind, I went into a business-like mode:

'We'll start with the police report. Perhaps we can track down the landlady. I have the address of the building.'

* * *

We managed to contact the landlady, who agreed to meet us in a café not far from where the building had burnt down. When asked if she remembered a tenant with a baby, she replied, 'I seem to recall a single woman living on the first floor called Theresa, but have no idea where she went. I was too busy retrieving my few remaining possessions from the burnt-down building to worry about my tenants, although some of them owed me money.'

Cleo and I took our leave from her, feeling downhearted.

'She wasn't much help, was she?' I commented.

'What should we do now?' asked Cleo.

'I know!' I said, 'We'll place an announcement in the Evening News and the local newspaper.'

Together, we drafted an ad which read:

'1944: BABY FOUND IN BURNT-DOWN BUILDING. 29 GRESHAM TERRACE. ANY INFORMATION PLS CONTACT BOX NO. ...'

'We don't want strange people knocking at our door!' I remarked.

'Oh Mummy! You think of everything!'

'We'll run them for a couple of weeks.'

I hoped that the search for Cleo's natural father would distract her from Harold's passing, just as Cleo had consoled me for the loss of my own baby.

At first we heard nothing. Then one day towards the end of a fortnight, a letter in a large official-looking envelope plopped onto the doormat. Cleo ran excitedly to pick it up. It was from the *Evening News*. Inside was a smaller envelope. Cleo wanted to tear it open but I made her wait while I picked up the letter-opener from the hall table. My hands were trembling as I unfolded the sheet of paper inside. At the top was an address in Leytonstone.

'Dear Sir or Madame,

I am replying to your advertisement in the *Evening News*. I lost a baby on 3rd September, 1944. I was living in the building that burnt down. I went out to do some shopping, and when I come back, the house was in flames.

Someone said that a woman had rushed in when she heard a baby crying, but neither she nor the baby were ever seen again.

Please tell me that my child is alive and well. I called her Anna.

Yours sincerely

Theresa James'

Cleo was so excited when she read the letter that she wanted me to go and see her straight away.

'No, I can't do that. She might be out and then I would have wasted a journey.'

I paused for thought.

'I'll write to her and tell her I'm coming.'

I looked up at the clock. 'If I can catch the 11 o'clock post, she should get it tomorrow morning.'

I wrote back, telling her that I believed her child was alive and well. I said I would come and visit her in two days' time. I gave her my phone number but I signed it with my maiden name just in case Theresa saw the stamp marked 'Chigwell' and looked me up in the telephone directory. I did not want a scene at the front door.

On Friday morning I set off for Leytonstone. It was raining heavily and I had to wait a long time for a bus.

Arriving at the front door of a three-storey block of flats, I rang the bell to Flat 2B. A breathless woman's voice came over the intercom.

'Who is it?'

'Lillian Maskel.'

I climbed up a flight of steps to the first floor. Looking along the tiled hallway, I noticed that one of the doors was open. A woman of about the same age as myself was standing on the threshold looking nervous and apprehensive. She was a couple of inches shorter than me, quite shapely, with a platinum bob of hair. She was smartly dressed in a red blouse and a black skirt with high heeled shoes.

'Good morning, Mrs Maskel. Please come in,' she said, stepping indoors to let me pass.

'Good morning Mrs. ... '

'Miss James,' she corrected me, lowering her lashes that were heavy with mascara.

I entered a small but bright bed-sit with a sofa bed and two chairs without arms at one end and a dining table and chairs at the other.

'Let me take your umbrella!'

Theresa motioned to the couch.

'Please, sit down! Would you like some tea?'

She disappeared into the kitchenette.

After I had removed my raincoat and settled down, I looked around the flat.

'Nice place you've got here!' I called out.

Now it was my turn to feel nervous as I contemplated how I was going to explain to this woman that I had stolen her baby.

Theresa came in bearing a tray.

'Yes, thank you. I was lucky to find it.'

She placed the tray on the coffee table, and with a shaking hand, poured the tea.

'So,' she began, looking at me earnestly, 'you have reason to believe that my child is alive and well?'

I sipped at my tea, which was scalding hot, so I put it down hastily.

Reaching for a carrier bag, I pulled out a carefully wrapped parcel. I opened it to reveal a faded lavender and pink shawl.

'Do you recognize this?'

Theresa gasped and opened her eyes wide as she stared at it in disbelief. Then she snatched it up and buried her face in it, breathing in deeply as if searching for her baby's fragrance. But it smelt of moth balls.

When she lifted her tear-stained face, she asked, 'Where did you find this?'

'Your baby was wrapped in it when I rescued her from the fire!' I replied.

Theresa stared at her.

'So you're the Mystery Woman!'

'Yes.'

Then I showed her the newspaper article. Theresa read it slowly, not quite able to take it in.

'So you saved my baby's life?'

'Yes!'

'I always knew that my baby was alive!' she exclaimed, bursting into a flood of tears. 'Thank you! Thank you for saving her life!'

When her sobs had died down, she sat quietly, sniffing and wiping her nose with a handkerchief. Then she looked up and added in a cold voice:

'But then you kept her for your own!'

'Yes. I didn't know what to do.'

'You never tried to find me? Until now?'

'It was a difficult time as you know during the war.' I paused, searching around for an excuse. 'I didn't know your name or where you had gone.'

'You could have tried the police!' she snapped back.

'I thought they might put her into an orphanage, along with hundreds of other lost or abandoned children! I did what I thought was best.'

After an awkward silence, I continued: 'Let me start at the beginning.'

I told Theresa how, after losing my own baby, I had rescued the child from the fire and had brought her up as my own.

Theresa stared at me the whole time, her mouth agape.

'You stole my child and robbed me of my happiness!' she burst out. 'Not a day goes by without me thinking of her!'

'I'm sorry. I know I did wrong but I saved her life.' I reached out to touch her hand. 'Can you find it in your heart to forgive me?'

Theresa lifted the soggy handkerchief that she was clutching and dabbed at her eyes.

For a minute she was unable to speak.

'Where is she now?' she finally blurted out. 'How is she? Is she well?'

'She's well and has grown into a lovely girl. She's 15 now, as you know.'

Theresa looked at me imploringly.

'Can I see her?'

'Of course! I'll bring her round tomorrow at the same time.'

I was relieved to see Theresa's face break into a joyful smile.

But I still had another question.

'Tell me something, is her father alive?'

'I don't know,' she replied.

Theresa heaved a sigh and gestured towards a framed photograph of a man in a Canadian Air Force uniform with thick dark hair like Cleo's.

'I was working as a barmaid in a club in Soho when I met Leonard. He would come in every night and stand by the bar drinking and talking to me. He asked me out but at first I refused. You can't be too sure with these overseas servicemen! Then one day he offered to take me to a dance on my day off and I agreed. He seemed like a decent sort of fella. After that I went out with him regularly after work. One day he gave me a ring that had belonged to his mother (it was a diamond surrounded by sapphires) and asked me to marry him. He was leaving for the war shortly and said he wanted to make sure of me before he went. I suppose I felt sorry for him, and in the end, I gave in to him. After he left, I found that I was expecting. I tried to write to him but I never heard from him again. I didn't tell anyone about the pregnancy. When it was beginning to show, I left my job, and when the time came gave birth on my own in the room. A few days later I needed to go out to buy some food and milk, so I left the baby alone for a few hours. I returned to find the building in flames. I tried to go in but the warden stopped me. I had lost everything – my home, such as it was, my baby, my possessions and clothes. I didn't want to spend the night in the underground station, so I went back to the club where I once worked and asked the boss if I could sleep on the leather couch for a couple of nights. He agreed – he was a decent chap. He lived upstairs with his wife and children, so he didn't bother me, although that wouldn't have stopped some men! After two days he gave me some money so that I could find a flat and buy myself some more clothes. He said that, if I would come back to work, he would deduct £2 from my wages every week until I had paid him back. I was devastated about losing the baby, but there was nothing much I could do about it. I always had the feeling that she was still alive, perhaps because of the story about the Mystery Woman.'

I commented on the fact that Theresa wasn't wearing her engagement ring.

'It is too precious. I might lose it. Besides,' she laughed, 'it might put the fellas off!.'

'Did you ever find out what happened to your fiancé?'

Her cheerful face dropped.

'I wrote to the Ministry of War about him. They told me that he was MIA – Missing in Action.'

She started to cry again.

I felt overwhelmed by a wave of sympathy for this woman who had lost everything during the war – her husband-to-be and her baby.

* * *

As I approached my house, I could see Cleo sitting in the bay window. Before I could open the gate, my daughter came rushing out through the front door and along the path.

'What happened?' she cried. 'Did you see her? What is she like? What did she say?'

'Just a minute dear, wait until I get my breath back!' I answered, making my way towards the kitchen where I put on the kettle.

When we were finally seated at the kitchen table with a pot of tea between us, I told her all that had taken place.

'And what about my father? Is he still alive?'

'Not as far as we know. According to the War Office he was missing in action, like a lot of men.'

Cleo started crying.

'Don't cry! After all, you never knew him.'

'That's the trouble!' she replied.

The next day Cleo was up and dressed before me, eager to meet her birth mother. I could tell she was both nervous and excited by the way that she picked at her breakfast.

When we arrived at Theresa's flat, we hardly had time to ring the bell when the door opened. Theresa must have been watching out of the window for our arrival. When she opened the door, Cleo stood in the threshold, staring at her, not sure what to do. I ushered her in. Theresa could contain herself no longer. She threw her arms around her long-lost daughter and gave her a hug, reluctant to let her go.

'I've dreamt of this moment for so long!' she exclaimed, wiping away the tears that trickled down her face.

'Sit down my dear and let me look at you!' she said, leading her to the couch. 'Of course, I knew you as Anna! And you've got your father's curly hair!'

She pointed to the photo of Leonard.

'Isn't he handsome?' she sighed. 'Oh listen to me, prattling on, forgetting my manners! Would you like a cup of tea?'

As soon as Theresa disappeared into the kitchenette, I moved over to the sofa and took Cleo's hand.

'Are you all right?'

Cleo looked confused and shaken.

'Yes. I'm just feeling a bit overwhelmed,' she replied, blinking back the tears.

When Theresa brought in the tea cups, I moved back to my chair.

As we were leaving, Theresa gave Cleo another hug, and then turned towards me.

'Thank you! Thank you for saving my daughter's life and bringing her back to me!' her wet cheeks were glowing with joy. 'This is the happiest day of my life!'

'And Cleo can come over and visit you whenever she wants to!' I replied with tears in my eyes, giving her a hug in turn.

* * *

When we reached home, I asked Cleo how she felt.

'I'm glad that I met her,' she answered thoughtfully. 'She seems like a nice lady.'

'I was afraid that you might want to go and live with her.'

I looked at her apprehensively.

'You'll soon be old enough to make your own decisions!'

'Oh no!' she replied, sliding her arm around my neck and kissing me on the cheek, 'You'll always be my Mummy!'

Queenager

(The word, 'queenager,' was added to the Oxford English Dictionary in 2024. It can be applied to a mature woman who dresses fashionably and has an active social life.)

My name is Betty Lou and I'm a queenager
I'm tall and slim and sassy. Now, where did I put my
    pager?

I wear the latest fashions (my clothes are á la mode)
My legs are long, my skirts are short, my face is like a
    toad!

My hair is blonde and wavy; not a grey hair in sight
But when I'm without make-up, I really look a fright!

My sister comes to visit me, now she's a great talker
We laugh and joke and have some fun! Where did I
    put my walker?

My head is in the clouds though my feet are in the
    basement
I love to dance and sing out loud in spite of hip
    replacement

I listen to pop music, especially when it's played
Upon a record player. Now, where is my hearing aid?

Although I'm getting on a bit, I notice men make
    passes
I often smile and flirt with them. Where did I leave
    my glasses?

My skin is all wrinkled and my teeth are not my own
But I'm still a queenager, though they call me an old
    crone

PART THREE

Living History

Life in La Herradura   199

Joaquim's Story   205

Maria   209

Paco and the Gypsies   213

Shipwreck in La Herradura Bay   215

A Poet of the People   221

The Sixties   227

LIVING HISTORY

While living in Spain, I had the privilege of being part of a group called 'The Culture Club.' The main purpose was to meet Spanish people, many of whom had grown up under Franco's dictatorship, to talk about their earlier lives. For many Spaniards, this was a rare occasion, because, as there had been atrocities committed by both the Nationalists and the Republicans, they had agreed to *un pacto de silencio* (a pact of silence). At first, most of our guests were nervous about discussing their experiences, conditioned by fear of retribution no doubt, until they realized that we were not there to judge them; our only interest was in hearing about life in Spain during those turbulent times. Then they started to relax and became more forthcoming.

I wish I could have interviewed the speakers in greater depth, but as they were speaking in Spanish, which was translated for us by one of the group leaders, it was as much as I could do to take scribbled notes.

The following stories come from a series that was published in *The Market Place*, under the title of 'Living History.' (Apologies to Hillary Clinton)

Life in La Herradura

Joachin, a teacher and plantation owner, started his talk by describing La Herradura in the days of his childhood.

During the 1940s and 50s, fishing and agriculture were the main industries. Because there was no money to spend on irrigation, the farmers grew crops such as olives, almonds and some kinds of grain that could survive in a dry climate.

Most of the land in the province of Málaga was owned by a rich family called Larios. The land in the Granada area belonged to an association of wealthy people. Most of the men living in the villages worked as day labourers. They would go to a central point and wait for a truck to come. The foreman would choose a handful of workers, and the rest would go home.

The villagers were so extremely poor that people would drop dead on the street from starvation.

Like many Lower Middle-Class people, he and his family lived in a building with a courtyard in the middle. In the centre of the patio there was a hole, and this is what the family would use as a toilet. There were no sewage pipes. Neither was there any running water. They had to fetch their daily supply from the pump. Many people kept animals in their courtyards.

A famous builder called Francesco Prieto Moreno lived in the area. As Director of Architecture, he oversaw the restoration of the Alhambra during Franco's time. Because he was a wealthy and generous man, he was able to donate a well to the village in 1965. The local people were grateful for his gift, and named streets after him to show their gratitude.

The poorest people lived at the top of the hill, farthest from the well. Their thatched houses were made of stones cemented together with dried mud.

In the 1960s a handful of tourists arrived from Madrid and other parts of Spain. They realized that it was a beautiful area with a sunny climate and began building holiday homes there. They were shortly followed by several wealthy Europeans and Americans, some of whom were famous. This was the start of tourism and hence the development of the construction industry, which brought a higher standard of living to the local people.

They built three hotels and several holiday homes in Almuñecar, which was more popular as a holiday resort than Nerja at that time.

After the building boom, when people had more money, some members of the association of the Granada province owners sold off much of their land, thus enabling the local farmers to become landowners. In Málaga, most of the land is still the property of the Larios family.

With the increase in wealth, they dug wells and pumped up water from the underground springs. With better irrigation, they were able to grow subtropical fruit such as avocados, mangoes and chirimoyas. Unfortunately, they drilled the wells too deeply, lower than sea level, so that the salt water from the Mediterranean came in and flooded the freshwater system. So they had to build reservoirs, which depended on rainfall and melted snow from the mountains. In recent years, the area has experienced heavy downpours, so that some of the water in the reservoirs had to be drained off, thus wasting a valuable commodity.

From the age of 14 to 23 years, Joachin lived in Málaga, where he completed his studies. In 1970, he moved to Ronda, where he worked as a teacher. He explained that the secondary school system in Spain has three tiers. There are the public (state run) schools, private schools, and a third sector called *centros concertados*, which are privately run schools paid for by the Government.

One of the members asked if the teachers had much freedom concerning what they taught. Joachin said that, in the 1970s, when Franco was in his declining years, the tight control of the previous decades became looser. Perhaps he was afraid that the younger generation and remaining Republicans would realize that the aging dictator only had a few years to live and might otherwise overthrow him, so the regime became more tolerant. Even the Guardia Civil, who had a reputation for brutality, were less aggressive. It was said of them, *'gritaba pero no mordía'* (they barked but they did not bite). Thus, democracy insinuated itself into the school system in the last years of dictatorship.

Joachin said that the teaching of religion was included in something called 'national spirituality,' which extolled the benefits of life in Spain under a dictatorship and taught the virtues of a good citizen. Sports, fitness and discipline were also on the curriculum. The recipients of this propaganda were 14 to 16-year-old boys. Girls learnt more domestic skills, such as sewing and cooking. Joachin explained that he went to camp in 1968 while he was at university in order to study 'national spirituality.' Without passing this subject, a student could not be awarded his or her degree.

Joachin added that the teaching of religion is no longer obligatory, and that it is paid for by the Church, not the Government.

On the subject of education for girls, Joachin said that at one time girls and boys were taught in separate schools. Ten years previous to his talk, integration had become obligatory in the state schools.

In response to a question, Joachin said that he taught Spanish and History. He had also worked with children with special needs. From 1973–75, he had been employed as the manager of a municipal company.

One of the members asked about his grandfather, who belonged to the socialist party. Joachin talked about the time when Málaga was under attack by Franco. Many civilians fled the city with what possessions they could carry, walking along the coast road towards Almeria. Many of them died on the way, most of them from fatigue or starvation, and some of them because they were on the road and therefore under fire from two directions; Italian planes strafed them from the air, and Germans attacked them from the sea. His grandfather arrived in Motril, where he was captured by the Nationalists. His family thought he would be taken for a *paseo*, or a little walk, meaning that he would be shot in the head. But instead they put him in prison for 5 months.

Joachin's mother and her sister were also socialists, and in danger of their lives.

During and after the Civil War, his family never spoke openly about politics, and the children were brought up to keep their mouths shut. People who criticized the regime were put to death. Every village was divided. There were people who had supported Franco, and others who were Republicans. They had killed each other, and for this reason there was real hatred between the two sides. They never discussed what had happened, but they did not mix.

He said that those who were wealthy or influential survived regardless of their political views.

Published in *The Market Place*
July 2011

Joaquim's Story

Joachim is a 75-year-old man whose father fought in the Civil War on the side of Franco. Joachim said that his father was not so much interested in politics, but whenever he saw people suffering, he felt impelled to go and help them.

At one point he was billeted in a village in the mountains. He was supposed to defend the villagers from looting, but many of the men who came down from the hills were soldiers from the other side just looking for food. His father was not afraid of dying, but he didn't want to fight for some trivial cause, so he went to the authorities and asked to be transferred.

While his father believed in the values of duty and honour, he was also something of a Don Juan. At one time he was courting three women in the same village, which was quite an achievement, even by Spanish standards! He did this by *saltar las tapias* or jumping over garden fences. Most of the houses had *rejas* or bars at the windows so that a man could approach a woman from the street or garden, while at the same time preserving her honour. The bars at Joachim's mother's house were wide apart, so that it was possible for the courting couple to kiss through them. One day, the woman's father caught them, but fortunately her parents were broad-minded. The father only commented jokingly, 'What? Are you leaving for Argentina? Is that why you are kissing my daughter goodbye?'

In the end, Joachim's father asked all three women to marry him, and his mother said yes. Apparently she was very beautiful.

Joachim was born at home, as there was no hospital nearby. His mother lost her first two babies soon after they were born. Joachim weighed 5.5 kilos (12 lbs!), but in spite of his hefty size, his mother was always afraid that he too would die, and was very protective of him.

When asked about his mother, Joachim said that she was like the sun. She had a flair for drama, so that if the local school needed some new books, she would put on a performance with the village people and charge a small admission, which she would then donate to the school or to another needy cause.

Joachim was trained as an electrical engineer. He worked as a teacher to older boys, but he found it difficult at first because there were behavioural problems. The boys would play about, shouting and throwing bits of paper around. Joachim hated his job, but could not leave, as it was his only means of financial support. One day in class, after there had been a moment of *rapprochement* with the boys, he said to them, 'You are mine, but more importantly, I am yours!' (At this point, Joachim became very emotional at the memory, and even shed a few tears.) After that moment he didn't have any more trouble with them. When the war came, many of the boys wanted to volunteer, but he told them that they should stay at school and finish their education. However, it was already too late, as most of them had already signed up. There was one boy who always sat at the front. He went off to fight, but survived, only to be run over by a car when he came back. This was a rare event as there was hardly any traffic on the road in those days. His mother was so grief-stricken that she could not accept his passing. She kept his room with his bed made up, as if he were going to return any day. Sadly, two years later, she could stand her sorrow no longer, and committed suicide by drinking bleach.

Joachim had fond memories of the postman who delivered the mail from his boyhood onwards. The mailman was an important person because he was a means of communication between the more remote villages. But he always did his job, regardless of the weather or the remoteness of the houses. He travelled on the bus, which had bad brakes, and there was one corner where the bus could not stop, so it would slow down and the postman would throw out the mail. When he got older, for some reason, the children used to make fun of him, but Joachim always held him in respect because he did his duty. Sadly, the bus driver failed to see him one day, and ironically the postman was run over by the very bus on which he had travelled most of his life. They found two donkeys and tried to take him to see a doctor, but he was dead before he arrived.

Someone asked Joachim what he thought about the modern world. He said that he regretted that traditional values were no longer taught or respected. He did not like the way young people dressed, and thought that too much emphasis was put on material wealth. He said that people had felt more stable during Franco's reign. They had a feeling of direction in their lives. Now he believed that young people had too much choice.

Published in *The Market Place*
April 2011

Maria

Maria was born into a wealthy family in Madrid. Her father worked for IBM and travelled the world. Her mother was closely connected with the political scene; she had worked with Primo de Rivera and is the cousin of Aznar, who was the leader of the centre right party and prime minister from 1996–2004. When asked about her father, Maria said she could not talk about him because it made her feel very emotional, but she was very close to him, and regarded him as the epitome of a heroic man.

When Franco died in 1975, Maria's mother was devastated, and it took her a long time to recover from the loss. When a member of the club asked her why her mother felt such devotion to Franco, she could not answer straight away. Then she said that the other side killed her grandmother's dog.

Her father was an only child, and his mother had doted on him. Even when he was an adult, if he was not feeling well, he would put on make-up to hide the pallor of his face before visiting her. When he married Maria's mother, the older woman found it hard to accept his new wife, and would find excuses to call him over to her house whenever she could. She would pretend there was an emergency, but when he arrived, there was no real problem. This was not always easy, as the younger couple lived on the outskirts of Madrid, and the mother lived in the centre. The mother looked down on all things Spanish, and denied being Spanish, although she was in fact born in Valencia.

When Maria was small, her family went to live in France, where Maria learnt to speak French fluently.

Eventually Maria's parents were divorced. At that time it was considered shameful, and Maria did not say anything about it to her friends at school. At the age of 17, Maria travelled with her father to Washington, DC, where she studied and learnt to speak English. She also met an artist, who became her husband. At a certain point, Maria decided to return to Spain without him, and they were later divorced. Because he was black, their two children had dark skin and curly hair. She met with a certain amount of prejudice when she came back to Spain.

When her father died, it changed her life. She inherited huge sums of money, but was devastated by grief at her loss.

She met a man of Peruvian background in Granada, and married him. She had two more children by him.

One of her younger girls was friendly with an eight-year-old German boy. He told her he could not be her boyfriend because of the colour of her skin. She pleaded with him, saying it was not her fault.

Maria separated from her second husband, and was forced to apply for social security. One of the men who was interviewing her treated her with contempt, unable to understand how a woman could have children by two men.

Now she lives in a *cortijo* (farmhouse) in the mountains without much in the way of material possessions. She said that she had grown up in a large house with everything that money could buy, but the house seemed empty and her parents were not happy. She realized that money did not buy happiness, and chose to live in a simpler way close to nature.

Published in *The Market Place*
February 2011

Paco and the Gypsies

Paco, a 50-year-old Spaniard, talked about his childhood and early years in Granada. His mother was a gypsy and lived in the Albaicín. She used to dance flamenco at the *zambra*, a meeting place for dancers and singers (named after the sound the instruments make). Several famous people came to watch her perform, including Anthony Quinn and Ingrid Bergman. Because the local people tended to look down on the gypsies, marriage between them was uncommon. The gypsies, who in turn preferred to keep to themselves, liked to 'marry their cousins.' But Paco's father was determined to marry the flamenco dancer, so he ran away with her to Lanjaron, where they got married. At first his parents found it hard to accept the young woman, but after a while they grew to love her and she became a welcome member of the family.

In 1960, Granada was affected by heavy rainstorms that destroyed many of the houses, particularly in the poorer quarter where Paco's family lived. The government, under Franco's rule, built new 2-bedroom houses for them, so Paco grew up in a modern house with his parents, sister and older brother.

Another of Franco's innovations was to build a railway system (RENFE) that connected all the major cities and larger towns, which all had their own train stations. Many of the buildings doubled as classrooms, so Paco went to school at the local railway station! Education was free for everyone.

A member of the audience asked Paco what he thought about Franco, but he said that his father forbad his family to talk about politics, sex or religion. There exists a general 'pact of silence' about the Spanish Civil War, in which neither side talks about the terrible things that happened.

Zapatero encouraged people to break this silence and to discuss the past, but Paco wouldn't spill the beans! He was born in 1960, 20 years after the Civil War, so his parents had no doubt already established a cult of silence on the subject.

The same member also asked him how people reacted to Franco's death. He said that the gypsies were grateful for the way in which he had helped them during the flood, when others might have ignored their plight. He described the transfer of power to Juan Carlos as a neatly tied package, with no loose ends. For this reason, it was a smooth transition.

Published in *The Market Place*
March 2011

Shipwreck in La Herradura Bay

25 SHIPS SINK IN LA HERRADURA BAY!
FIVE THOUSAND PEOPLE PERISH AT SEA

These might have been the headlines in a Spanish newspaper 450 years ago, when half the Spanish navy was destroyed in a storm. Very little documentation remains of this tragic event, which is why Tomás Hernández, award-winning poet and novelist, has written a book about it.

From 1588 to 1604, the Spanish fleet was engaged, alongside other European countries, in fighting the Turks. This powerful navy was sometimes referred to as the *Armada Invencible*. Sr. Hernandez started his talk by pointing out that the fleet destroyed in La Herradura was not part of the invincible army, as the events took place 25 years earlier, in 1562.

The armada at the time was divided in two parts: half patrolled Genoa and Naples in an attempt to control the Mediterranean, the other half travelled from Valencia and Málaga to North Africa, where they visited Spanish colonies. Out of 28 ships, 25 were destroyed in the space of 4 to 5 hours. In this short period, 5,000 people died in a 2½ km. area. The last 3 boats escaped damage because they were not able to round the cape (la Capa de la Mona) into the bay.

On the fateful day of 18th October, a fleet of galleys left Málaga bound for Oran, carrying soldiers to replace those already stationed in Algeria. One soldier complained to the captain, Don Juan de Mendoza, because it was late in the year, and not a safe time to cross the Mediterranean, but they had to exchange the soldiers, so the trip took place.

The galleys were small flat narrow boats, 60 metres long and 6 metres wide, powered by sails and oarsmen. A replica can be seen in the *Museu Marítim* in Barcelona, which was formerly a ship-building yard. There were 20 oars on either side of the boat, 8–12 metres in length and each weighing between 100 and 150 kilos. They were so large and heavy that they required four men per oar. In addition to 200 oarsmen, each ship carried 15 to 20 riflemen, 35–45 infantry, sailors to crew the boat, specialists to repair the oars, candle-makers, a drummer to synchronize the rhythm of the oarsmen, and horses. (No chickens were carried on board because they became seasick and died.) Sr. Hernández asked himself how so many people and animals could be crammed on board such a small boat. The prow or poop deck was reserved for the captain, and there was only a 60 cm. walkway between the oarsmen. The rowers were prisoners (the word for a prisoner is *galeote*) and were chained to their seats day and night. They would eat where they sat, and a tent was constructed over them to give them shelter from the rain. If a fight broke out, they were given a ration of rum and bacon to calm them down. The average lifespan of an oarsman was 4 years. Life started at dawn, when they swabbed the decks. As there was no water available for washing, the men gave off a strong body odour. It was said that you could smell a galley coming at night long before you could see it!

In addition to the crew and soldiers, the ships were laden with food.

Many of the boats contained women and children, the families of soldiers who were going to visit their relatives. The death of two small children going to visit their father, the Governor of Oran, was reported in the chronicles of the time.

At 10 o'clock the following morning, the fleet sailed into the bay at La Herradura, where the ships sought shelter from an easterly wind. They dropped anchor and waited for the storm to pass. Suddenly an unexpected southerly wind blew in from Africa, causing a violent storm. The boats, anchored too closely to one another, were jostled by the wind and waves, and crashed against each other, causing them to break up and sink.

Fortunately, Captain Mendoza had 'commanded to let loose the galley slaves and gave order to the other galleys to do the same,' so the oarsmen were released from their chains when the boats were shaken by the first wind, giving them the opportunity to escape. But the chances of survival were small, as they were likely to be crushed by the sides of the boats as they smashed into each other. One captain was hit on the head by a piece of wreckage. In all, only eight captains survived.

Two days after the shipwreck had occurred, Captain General Luis de Mendoza, who was the uncle of the naval captain, went to inspect the extent of the damage. He said that the bay was full of dead people from one side to the other.

Sr. Hernández was curious to find out where they were all buried. The storm took place in October, but the bodies that were buried in Velez Malaga did not arrive until November or December. There was another storm the following March which uncovered some of the bodies on the beach. They were buried again with the help of the local people.

Very little documentation of the shipwreck has been found. The Governor of Melilla in North Africa was the godfather of a Jew who had converted to Christianity. On the convert's baptismal certificate, he had written after his signature that he was a survivor of the shipwreck. A man from the Basque country called Martin de Figueroa moved to Italy, where he later died. During his stay, he wrote a letter to his family referring to the disaster. Philip II, who was a bureaucrat, kept records that are stored in Barcelona.

The most detailed record that remains is an epic poem of 420 verses describing the tragic events. It was written by a soldier, who had tried to emulate the style of a classic writer of epic works. From the point of view of literary merit, it is not a great poem, but it was written in his spare time and is a first-hand record of the disaster. It was also an elegy (a *cante de muerte*) that immortalized those who had lost their lives. It must have been painful for him to relive those horrific events. The poem was published in 1881, but 14 or 15 lines were left out. It was not an independent edition, but part of a larger publication, so there was nothing that could be done about it. Professor Carmen Calero, a teacher in the Medieval History Department at the University of Granada, published it again in 1991. Sr. Hernández took most of his information from this poem.

Another mystery was the fact that not many remains of the boats were found. Perhaps pieces had been salvaged in the past and reused. A Swedish man had an anchor that his mother had found in the 1960s. Several bars in Almuñecar displayed parts that were said to have been stolen from the ships. In Punta de la Mona, two large anchors were exhibited, but they turned out to be fakes.

Professor Calero went on a diving trip to see if she could find any wreckage under the sea, but the organizers of the excursion were not serious about doing any research.

The only memorial is a bronze statue in La Herradura.

Published in *The Market Place*
September 2011

Miguel Hernández – A Poet of the People

On 27th March, 2011 the members of the Cultural Club visited Rosario Gonzalez's art studio in La Herradura to attend an *homage* to Miguel Hernández, one of the most influential poets to emerge from the Spanish Civil War.

The art studio was set in a *finca* in the middle of town – a house with a plot of land where fruit and vegetables grow, the only one of its kind in the area. We entered through the studio, where Rosario's work was on display, and passed into an enchanting walled garden, where we sat down under an orange tree that was already in bloom. The fragrance of the blossoms was intoxicating. Bunches of green mangoes hung in clusters on a nearby tree. Perfumed jasmine cascaded down the wall and freesias grew at our feet.

A Siamese cat passed amongst the guests and allowed herself to be stroked before settling in a warm spot dappled with sunlight and shade.

As the poetry reading began, a cockerel started crowing itself hoarse, drowning out any hope of hearing what was being said. Fortunately, we had been given a print-out in Spanish and English beforehand, so we were able to follow the reading. When it was finished, we left the garden to enjoy a glass of sangria in the artist's studio, where we had a chance to admire her watercolours and oil paintings. The whole experience was truly magical.

* * * * *

Hernández was born in Orihuela in the Province of Valencia into a poor family. Growing up, he worked as a goatherd and farmhand. He was mostly self-taught, having had little formal training beyond the basic education that he received at state schools and under the Jesuits.

Influenced by European vanguard movements such as Surrealism, he became part of a generation of Spanish authors concerned about workers' rights.

In 1933 he met Josefina Manresa Marhuenda in Orihuela, whom he married in 1937. She became the inspiration for his romantic poems. In December 1937, she gave birth to a son, who died 10 months later. In January 1939, their second son was born.

Unable to flee the country at the end of the Civil War, Hernández was arrested several times for his anti-fascist sympathies. He was eventually condemned to death as 'an extremely dangerous and despicable element to all good Spaniards.' Franco later reduced the death sentence to a 30-year prison term for fear of him becoming a martyr like the poet, Lorca. He spent the rest of his life in various jails living under extremely harsh conditions, until he died of tuberculosis in 1942.

While in prison, he produced an extraordinary amount of poetry, which he called *Cancionero y Romancero de Ausencia* (Songs and Ballads of Absence). The poet wrote not only about the Spanish Civil War and his imprisonment, but of the death of his infant son and the struggle of his wife and second child to survive poverty. He also uses imagery from the soil.

The following is an excerpt from *Vientos del Pueblo* (Winds of the People) by Miguel Hernández, written in1937:

Winds of the People

The winds of the people lift me up,
The winds of the people sweep me along,
They bring joy to my heart
And air to my lungs

Oxen bow their foreheads
Meek and impotent in the face of punishment;
Lions raise their heads, and at the same time
Inflict punishment with their clamouring claws

I am not from a people of oxen,
But from people who seize
Ancient settlements of lions
High passes of eagles
And mountain ranges of bulls
With pride as their flag.
Oxen never thrived
On the bleak plateaux of Spain

Who said you could throw a yoke
Around the neck of this race?
Who can hobble or yoke a hurricane?
Or who can cage lightening like a prisoner in a jail?

If I die, may I die
With my head held high
Dead and twenty times dead,
My mouth against the wild grass,
I will have my teeth clenched
And my jaw resolute

* * * * *

Singing, I await death
For there are nightingales that sing
Above the guns
And in the midst of battle.

Vientos del Pueblo

Vientos del pueblo me llevan,
Vientos del pueblo me arrastran,
me esparcen el corazón
y me aventan la garganta.

Los bueyes doblen la frente,
Impotentemente mansa, delante de los castigos:
los leones la levantan
y al mismo tiempo castigan con su clamorosa zarpa

No soy un de pueblo de bueyes,
que soy de un pueblo que embargan
yacimientos de leones,
desfiladeros de àguilas
y cordilleras de toros
Con el orgullo en el asta.
Nunca medraron los bueyes
en los paramos de España.

¿Quién habló de echar un yugo
sobre el cuello de esta raza?
¿Quién ha puesta al huracán jamas ni yugos ni
    trabas,
Ni quién al rayo detuvo prisionero en una jaula?

Si me muero, que me muera
con la cabeza muy alta.
Muerto y veinte veces muerto,
la boca contra la grama,
tendré apretados los dientes
y decidida la barba.

* * * * *

Cantando espero a la muerte,
que hay ruiseñores que cantan
encima de los fusiles
Y en medio de las batallas.

LAST BUT NOT LEAST!

The Sixties

(My personal contribution to Living History!)

On the rare occasions that I have brought up the subject of the '60s with Spanish men, I have always had the same response – 'Oh, yes. Free love!'

It is not surprising that this is the main aspect that they have seized upon, having lived under the iron grip of Franco and the Catholic Church. The music, the colour, the freedom and the revolutionary nature of that magical decade must have seemed like a distant psychedelic dream to them.

The truth, in my opinion, is that there is no such thing as free love – someone has to pay, and it's usually the woman. Out of about 20 girls in my mixed class, there were only three who had actually 'gone all the way' and we all knew who they were – Mary, Bess and Hilary. I shall say no more. Although we came of age during the Sixties, we had of course grown up in the Fifties. Our parents had taught us to wait until we were married, unless we wanted the shame of an unplanned pregnancy. So most of us behaved ourselves. With the Advent of the Pill, things certainly changed, and no doubt the numbers of young people experimenting with sex increased as the decade progressed.

When the Beatles were singing, 'She was just 17,' so was I. One of the Sixth Form boys invited me to a party. There were no drugs available to us at that time (1962) as they were considered the domain of artists and intellectuals and hadn't filtered down to our level of society. There was very little alcohol either, because we were not working and only had our pocket money. So what did we do? We danced to the music! I remember twisting to Chubby Checker ('Let's do the Twist') and the Beatles ('Twist and Shout'). Trad jazz was also popular amongst us (Acker Bilk and Chris Barber). One of the boys taught me how to stomp, and when we danced we cleared the floor. Not that I was such a good dancer, although my partner was. Part of the dance entailed rotating your free arm in a horizontal direction from the elbow. We could build up quite a speed, and if you combined the forearm swing with a swift turn of the body through 360°, you could create enough momentum to knock someone flying if they got in the way.

When we weren't dancing, we would sit around and talk, as students do. The popular subjects of the time were Communism, the hydrogen bomb, the Apartheid system in South Africa, the Meaning of Life and the Existence of God. And yes, there was some smooching!

I loved classical music, and I also liked gospel, jazz and the blues. I used to play Sonny Boy Williamson on my brother's homemade record player. Although we had similar tastes in music, he was more particular about the technical aspect of a recording. He said it sounded like bacon frying.

It all started with Elvis in the Fifties. As John Lennon said, 'Before Elvis, there was nothing.' Then Bill Haley and his kiss curl brought us 'Rock around the Clock' and everybody started jiving. It had an exciting rhythm and it was easy to dance to, but Bill was no pop idol.

Then came the Beatles. The earth shifted on its axis, and everything changed. Their first record, 'Love me do,' caused a tsunami of excitement that ran through the teenage population of the time. After that, one single followed another, each song as good as, if not better than, the previous. We knew we were witnessing something exceptional.

Nowadays we have Celebrities. In the Sixties we had Superstars: John Lennon, Paul McCartney, Mick Jagger, Jimi Hendrix, Bob Dylan, Eric Clapton. I would include Joan Baez, who had a voice that would silence nightingales. She helped to promote Bob Dylan. When she was performing, she would always invite him onto the stage. When he was on the stage, he would never invite her. Discouraged, she returned to Sacramento. The list extended to other creative people, such as Rudolph Nureyev, who defected from Russia in 1963, dazzling Margot Fonteyn and the rest of us with his leaps and pirouettes. Princess Margaret and her dashing boyfriend/husband, Anthony Armstrong Jones, added sparkle and glamour. In the art world there was Andy Warhol, amongst others.

Then there were those who may not be classed as Superstars, but were still outstanding singers, musicians and performers. In America there were the Everly

Brothers, Buddy Holly, Chuck Berry, the Temptations, the Beach Boys and Crosby, Stills & Nash. The women included Joni Mitchel, Carol King, Carly Simon, Janis Joplin and Aretha Franklin.

In addition to solo artists, Phil Spectre and his 'Wall of Sound' promoted many female groups such as the Shirelles, Diana Ross and the Supremes and Martha and the Vandellas.

In England we had, in addition to the Beatles and the Rolling Stones, Eric Burden and The Animals, Joe Cocker, Rod Stewart, the Bee Gees, Elton John, Herman and the Hermits, the Dave Clark Five and Alan Price. The list goes on and on. If I've missed anyone out, it isn't surprising.

With the sunburst of music came a change in fashion. Carnaby Street and Kings Road became psychedelic shopping centres. If you wanted a dimly lit emporium with a woman in a full-length dress playing a grand piano on an upper floor while you sipped afternoon tea, and a garden on the roof, you could go to Biba's in High Street Ken. I once bought a black sweater with a red heart on the sleeve. When I got it home, I realized it was navy blue! They exchanged it for me. Twiggy was the fashion icon, and with her came short skirts. They became shorter and shorter, until it became embarrassing to sit down. I was relieved when the midi *a la* 'Bonnie and Clyde' became popular. In the early Sixties we wore our hair in a beehive, which entailed copious back-combing and lacquer. Vidal Sassoon came to our rescue with sensational cuts that went with the natural wave or curl of the hair, needing very little to keep it in place.

In the mid-Sixties my friend and I used to go to clubs in London. Ronnie Scott's in Oxford Street and the Marquee were our favourites. One day, a young black man appeared on the stage, which was only about 8 inches above floor level, and introduced a new song that had only just come out. It was called 'Respect' and the artist was James Brown. The place wasn't very crowded so Jackie and I had plenty of room to jigger about in front of the stage. It had a good beat and was easy to dance to. When he had finished the audience clapped politely. Little did we know that it would become the anthem of the Civil Rights Movement in America.

After I finished College, I moved back to London and shared a flat with three other women, one of whom was an American. A stream of her friends appeared at our door wanting to sleep on our sofa in the living room. That's how I was introduced to drugs. The first time I smoked marijuana (or was it hashish? I can't remember) I felt pleasantly high and giggled a lot. Her friend suggested we go to see a film called 'Monterey Pop,' which was playing locally. That is how I came to watch Janis Joplin sing 'Ball and Chain' in a gold lamé dress.

Although I was offered other drugs, I never took them. I was told that LSD could bring on schizophrenia if you had a tendency towards it, which I thought I probably did. While some people had ecstatic spiritual experiences, others had bad trips accompanied by terrifying hallucinations from which there was no return. I never touched hard drugs. Of course, there were casualties amongst those who overdosed. Sadly, we lost many bright stars, Janis Joplin and Jimi Hendrix amongst them. The truth is that nearly everybody took drugs in those days. Those who deny it were probably too stoned to remember. The problem was that the Mafia realized that drugs were a highly lucrative commodity, and started increasing the potency of relatively soft drugs like marijuana or lacing them with stronger chemicals in an attempt to promote addiction.

The Sixties was a time of revolution, and several major changes took place politically. There was a war in Vietnam, which was dragging on, and America, with all her military power, seemed unable to bring it to an end. Young American men were forced to join up, to fight the 'Geeks and Commies' on the other side of the world. What they did not know at the time was that the Vietnamese had an underground network of tunnels where they could retreat and hide when in danger. The war was an unpopular one, and demonstrations took place all over the United States and in England too, to the accompaniment of 'We shall Overcome.' When soldiers returned to the US, stunned, having seen their friends killed or having been obliged to kill people they did not know, expecting a hero's welcome, they would be booed and jeered at.

My friends persuaded me to take part in a peaceful demonstration outside the American Embassy on Grosvenor Square. We arrived and took our places in front of a wall of police on horseback, bearing shields and truncheons. The crowds amassed behind us and someone at the back yelled out, 'Push!' I was forced forward until I was at eye-level with a horse's chest. In the tussle that followed, I lost a shoe and was caught off balance. I nearly fell over, but was held aloft by the crush of the crowds around me. I knew that if I fell, I might be trampled, either by the demonstrators or, worse still, the horses. One of the policemen (God bless British Bobbies!) saw I was in trouble, and helped me off to the side. I limped home on the Underground with only one shoe.

The end of the war came in 1972, speeded up, I would like to think, by the demonstrations that took place against it.

Other ground-breaking changes were taking place, both in the UK and America. Thanks to the leadership of Martin Luther King, the Civil Rights Act was passed in 1964, which made discrimination based on skin colour illegal; the Voting Rights Act of 1965 gave black people, many of whom had fought in the Vietnam war, the right to vote. King was assassinated in April 1968. Up until the time of his death, both black and white people had joined forces in the protest marches. After his passing, there seemed to be a cooling off in the attitude of black people towards white Americans who might normally have supported them in their struggle. As one Black Panther explained to Louis Theroux, 'If you see a hundred snakes coming towards you, you don't stop and think, 'Oh, this snake is harmless, that snake is poisonous.' You just run from them all.'

The anti-war demonstrations and the Civil Rights marches led to the counter-culture group in America known as the Hippies. Its members were for the most part middle class, who rejected the mores of their parents. They were characterised by their love of rock music, sexual freedom and the use of psychedelic and other drugs. Both men and women wore their hair long, usually parted in the middle. They dressed in jeans or long flowing kaftans with strings of coloured beads or long silk scarves around their necks. Janis Joplin promoted the use of feather boas.

The Women's Liberation Movement, which also started in America, brought about more important changes. A group of about 60 men and women had gone to a remote part of Colorado to set up a commune. When they arrived, there was only one large hut, which was used for cooking, eating and sleeping. With men and women sharing the same dormitory area, they began to pair off. Soon the men drew up a list of rules (perhaps the ones who weren't getting as much attention as they would have liked): the women were not allowed to sleep with one partner more than twice in a row. The result was chaos; it was difficult to sleep with the screams of women being raped every night, which was when the women got together and decided upon their own set of rules. Thus began the Women's Liberation Movement, in which women claimed the right to decide what happened to their own bodies. It wasn't about burning bras, although some protested against wearing restrictive underwear.

The movement soon spread to England, and again manifested itself in important legislation. With the spread of the permissive society, many women, who had for some reason not availed themselves of the Pill, found themselves expecting a child they were not able or prepared to care for. As a result of protests, the Abortion Act was passed in 1967. Although many people may have reservations about terminating a pregnancy, I think that legal abortion was preferable to illegal abortion.

The other legislation that had a great effect on women's lives was Equal Pay for Equal Work.

In 1968 the machinists at the Dagenham Ford Factory went on strike to demand pay at the same rate as men. Their actions brought the car plant to a standstill. The movement affected women all over Britain and then spread to other countries around the world. As a result, the Equal Pay Act of 1970 was the first piece of legislation in the UK to mandate economic parity between men and women in the workplace.

In May of the same year, French students in Paris put up barricades and took control of the city.

The anti-war demonstrations, the Civil Rights activists and the Women's Liberation Movement inspired the Gay Liberation Front that emerged at the end of the Sixties. In the UK, homosexual behaviour between consenting adults was decriminalized in 1967.

In August 1969, a rock festival took place in a small town called Woodstock. People flocked from miles around and started pushing down the wire netting that surrounded the area. In the end the promoters, who were unable to control the crowds, declared it a free concert. It lasted three days and during most of that time it rained. People started taking off their clothes, which were too wet to give them any protection from the elements, and started sliding about in the mud. For those who kept their clothes on, jeans were *de rigour*. A handful of people overdosed or had bad trips from drugs, but for all that there was no reported violence. Woodstock is remembered for its outstanding musical performances and a feeling of *camaraderie* amongst participants. As one policeman commented, if you were to put a large crowd of men together and they were all drinking alcohol, they would have all been at each other's throats by now.

On 6th December, 1969, the Rolling Stones held a concert in Altamont. They hired Hell's Angels as security guards. As the Stones started playing 'Sympathy for the Devil,' a young black man called Hunter moved to the front of the stage. The Angels persuaded him to move further back. He retreated but he was in a rage and returned wielding a pistol. A Hell's Angel stabbed him and then he was beaten to death. That was the end of the Sixties.

The Beatles broke up in 1970. John and Paul pursued solo careers, but somehow it was never the same.

It was a tumultuous time, exploding with music, creativity and the spirit of revolution; one that I would not have missed for the world.

I wish you all Love, Peace and Rock and Roll!

Acknowledgements

I would like to extend my gratitude to all my friends and fans who have encouraged me to write over the years. In particular I would like to thank Marilyn Barry, author of the *Rachel Spring Trilogy*, who read through *Pawz* for any glaring mistakes.

About the Author

Janet.Patterson was born in Cambridge, grew up in the suburbs of London and went on to study English and Drama at college, which she later taught at secondary school level. She then became a teacher of English as a foreign language, which enabled her to travel and work abroad.

Her itchy feet soon led her to the South of France, where she studied French and taught English for two years.

Upon her return to England, she found employment at an English Language school in Oxford. The following year she took a course in Business Studies at Oxford Brookes.

In 1976 her nomadic life took her to New York, where she worked at the Ford Foundation.

Her love for adventure led her to Russia while it was still behind the Iron Curtain, Lapland, where she slept in a Lap hut within the Arctic Circle and India, where she stayed on an Ashram.

Ms. Patterson now lives in Spain, where she has fulfilled her life-long ambition of becoming a writer. She has published two books of short stories entitled *Al Gore goes to Heaven* and *Mme. Wadjinski's Magic Mirror* and is currently working on a family history with the pretentious title of *Corbets and Kings*.

www.ingramcontent.com/pod-product-compliance
Lightning Source LLC
Chambersburg PA
CBHW022156260626
47155CB00019B/3055